PRAISE

"A cabinet of marvels and curiosities await you in Elad Haber's debut, The World Outside. From fairy tales to fabulism, and scifi to dark fantasy, you'll encounter a spectrum of the strange and delightful here. Haber's vision gazed toward the world outside, but there are many worlds to explore inside these pages. You won't regret the trip."
  —Christopher Barzak, Shirley Jackson Award winning author of Before and Afterlives.

"Haber's short stories always have a music to them, that draws you along as you plumb the startling depths of the human heart, in fairy tales and futures and sometimes a present-day that's been revealed to you with fresh eyes."
  —Jennifer R. Donohue, author of Exit Ghost

"Every single story in Elad's collection is like a finely cut gem. The prose is fantastic and sharp, and the imagination is like a rare jewel in my mind. These will be stories I treasure and return time and again, for years to come, for they already haunt me with their beauty."
  —Paul Jessup, author of The Skinless Man Counts to Five

"A wide-ranging, highly-enjoyable collection of fantastic fiction!"
  —Daniel Braum, author of The Night Marchers and Other Strange Tales

THE WORLD OUTSIDE

stories by

ELAD HABER

Underland Press

The World Outside is a collection of fictional stories. Names, characters, places, and incidents are the products of the individual author's imagination or are used in an absolutely fictitious manner. Any resemblance to actual events, locales, or persons—living or dead—is entirely coincidental.

Text Copyright © 2024 by Elad Haber

Extended copyright information may be found on page 192.

All rights reserved, which means that no portion of this publication may be reproduced or transmitted, in any form or by any means, without the express written permission of the publisher.

This book is published by Underland Press, which is part of Firebird Creative, LLC (Clackamas, OR).

You have no idea what the world used to be like . . .

Edited by John Klima
Book Design and Layout by Firebird Creative

This Underland Press trade edition has an ISBN of 978-1-63023-080-7.

Underland Press
www.underlandpress.com

THE WORLD OUTSIDE

For my fathers.

Table of Contents

Foreword 1

i.
Ophelia and The Beast 5
A Beauty, Sleeping 10
Rapunzel Goes Mad 14
Doll Parts 16

ii.
Number One Hit 24
Do What You Desire 37
The Conductor Sighs 48
Time Keep 51

iii.
It Only Rains at Night 60
D 73
Bee Mine 87
Stay in Your Homes 89

iv.
But My Heart Keeps Watching 102
Halfway Down the Hole 112
Never Stop Moving 116
The Dying Disease 128
Young Man, Are You Lost? 135

v.

Life in a Glasshouse 143
The Remembrance Engine 156
All My Memories Are You 167
A Fiery Lull 175

Acknowledgments 191
Bibliography 192
Biography 195

Foreword

The assembled stories mark twenty years of publishing fiction, highlighted here with eighteen of my publications in the science fiction, fantasy, horror, and literary fiction markets as well as three unpublished stories. The published stories were featured in various print and online magazines from 2003 to 2023. I have realized in my writing that I often return to similar themes: homes and homelessness, grief, music, and narcotics. I have grouped the stories in this collection into thematic quartets and octets to further explore these throughlines in my work.

A couple of days before my high school's graduation in 1998, I boarded a plane from New York City to East Lansing, Michigan, to attend the Clarion East Writer's Workshop. I was one of two eighteen-year-olds in the class. There were a few college age people, but most of the group was older. It was an incredible six weeks where I made life long friendships and my progress as a young writer was accelerated beyond just craft and technique. Most of the class published immediately, both short stories and novels. But not me.

I remained unpublished throughout my years in college, despite many attempts. And this was back when you couldn't just email a submission. The allusive Acceptance seemed ever more like a fantasy.

It was only when I moved back to the East Coast and took the Magical Jewish Train that whisks New Yorkers to Miami like a Star Trek teleporter that I started to publish. In the early days of online magazines, I was able to place a few stories at pindelyboz.com, an early progenitor of what has become a huge online marketplace.

But I was burnt out. My mountain of rejections and so many discarded manuscripts took a world-weary toll and I needed time away. I didn't write anything for years.

But then I married my best friend, my amazing wife, Shawn, and she settled me down and helped me get over so many personal losses and disappointments, that I felt like I could get back into writing. To find my creative outlet and try to use it to entertain and enlighten readers.

One of the first stories I wrote when I returned to writing is the centerpiece of this collection, "Number One Hit," which was my also first professional sale. It is the story of a world after this one, where relics like art and music are stolen with often violent means in a post apocalyptic Las Vegas.

Elsewhere in these stories, there is my science fiction take on the haunted house trope, a story about a superhero that lives on the moon, a global spanning stargazing journey, a near future retelling of Adam and Eve, twisted versions of fairytales and ghost stories, a story of a girl so broken hearted by the loss of her dad, that she would do anything to get a piece of him back and a future so hot, it's deadly to be outside.

Enjoy the journey.

Ophelia and the Beast

Hark! Hear the maiden's cry as she drowns herself. A gurgle on the face of the water. A single splash. An asphyxiated sound, cut off mid-choke. Engulfing darkness. The sound of rushing water.

The river rumbles with anger at the intrusion. The pressure presses on her, squeezes her body, grips her lungs like a God crushing a mortal.

Death, a whisper. *So, this is what it feels like.*

She dies . . . She dies with a look of shock: an open mouthed gape, raised eyebrows, cheeks pulled in, about to yell. As if any of this is a surprise.

*

Her body, flotsam, glides along Moses-like, half-submerged. A head or arm or leg roll and show themselves, only to get smacked by a rock, or tangled in seaweed and capsized again. Relaxed-looking fish circle and dodge her, laughing and biting at the dead human.

Ha, ha, ha, says the Fish.

*

She floats and floats. For how long? Who knows? Centuries, maybe. Through realities and mythologies and minds and hearts and . . .

*

Finally, she comes aground, on a small, lonely shore, surrounded in all directions by forest, dense and dark.

A form rushes out of the wilderness and towards the maiden. It is huge, blocking out the moon at times. (A bear?) It runs on four legs and emits a nasty scent-of-a-thousand-men smell. The beast sniffs at the dead girl, tries to nudge her awake. He uses a furry paw to push aside a stalk of wet hair, like a thin, dead leech, stuck to her face.

Little bites and scratches cover her skin, the color of the river, blue-green. Her eyes, large, brown, but vacant, retain some essence of who she was. Intelligence, compassion in those eyes, sadness too. The creature stares at her for a long time.

Then, as sudden as a miracle, the beast scoops her up in two arms and runs back into the forest. On two legs!

*

A mansion hidden in the woods. All the fixings of royalty: crests and halls lined with portraiture, banners and frescos depicting family trees; all the makings of civilization: kitchens, bedrooms, indoor-bathrooms, closets full of clothes, carpeting everywhere; but with all the life of a desert in the harshest heat of summer. Take a step, it'll echo for a week. Touch a wall, the print will stick like glue.

The front door is smacked open and the Beast, carrying the girl, scamper inside. He drops her, rushing water pouring out of *his* fur and *her* body and making a waterfall for her to fall into.

The Beast, his shoulders wide as the base of a tree, falls to his knees beside the girl and begins a crude CPR on her: breathing into her lungs without the help of any chest-pumps. How he knows the technique, we'll never know for certain; ask him and he'll *say*, "Knowledge is as timeless as I am."

The girl, thoroughly dead, makes no response to his efforts, but the Beast continues in his steady work. A faint glow emanates from his chest, centered on his heart. It glows and pulses, changing shape and gaining volume, resembling an animated fractal pattern. The Beast continues his work, unabated, huffing. The ball of light passes from the Beast into the girl, encapsulates her in faint light. Her body changes color, violent reds and blues first, then returns to its pinkish roots. The scratches and bites foam and disappear; her hair dries, takes shape and color and texture. She coughs, once, twice, then opens her eyes.

A gasp from both parties.

Upon seeing the creature above her, the maiden screams as loud as she can. It echoes for a month.

✱

"Ophelia," says the Beast, speaking emphatically to a wooden door. "Won't you come out? Won't you let me talk to you, help you? You're grieving, I understand. You're grieving for him... for Hamlet, but you have to realize, you have to understand..."

The double doors shudder in response and are flung open. Ophelia, dressed in a black gown, her raven hair tied back in a ponytail, her puffy eyes spilling black makeup all over her cheeks.

"Don't *you* speak his name!" she shouts, malice in her vowels. "*You* don't have the right . . . *Creature!*"

She slams the doors. (Echo, echo, echo.)

✱

Once, long ago, there may have been servants.

Now, there is dust everywhere. On the countertops and the statues, the chairs and even the fireplace. Footprints, paw-shaped, are ghost-like on the floors. And *that smell*. Oldness. Death. Inactivity.

Activity, now: the Beast in the kitchen, assembling lunch for the lady of the house. He's slow and methodical in his work, huge shoulders hunched over as he concentrates on cutting a piece of cheese with a knife designed for a human. He fumbles and slices a gash into his palm, right beside the echo of another. His growl is quick, annoyance not anger.

He doesn't mind cooking.

When he brings the dish up to Ophelia's room, he pauses in front of the door and, as usual, waits. Sometimes he takes the dish off the meal and lets the smell of roasted lamb or fresh fruit linger in the air, through the gaps in the doorframe. Hoping, all the while.

It's been two months. They've spoken only a paragraph to each other. And a short one, at that.

When Ophelia doesn't come out to greet him (which is not once, yet), the Beast lays the platter on the floor, picks up the empty dish from breakfast, and walks away.

✱

Three months. Agonizingly long. Living with someone and not talking is perplexing, unnatural, destructive. The air so thick with silence, Ophelia's moans and cries echo and intensify . . . to the Beast, sitting alone in his library-sanctuary. More and more often, lately, the Beast has spent whole nights in the surrounding woods, hunting for food for himself and Ophelia. For the first time in his long, long life, he feels uncomfortable in his own mansion.

In his usual chair he sits, now. Besides a rain-speckled window, he reads by candlelight from a hundred scattered candelabra across the wide room. The shadows cast by a thousand individual flames play hide-and-seek on the bookshelves, the muraled ceiling, the decorative carpeting.

The Beast looks up from his book, sniffs. A hesitant knock sounds at his door. At the second, louder knock, the Beast springs up and dashes to it in a flash. (You would have had no idea he could move so fast.)

He grabs two lion-head-shaped doorknobs in his paws and opens the double doors. She stands in the center, framed Venus-like, in a white gown, familiar to the Beast.

Ophelia curtsies and says, "Gracious Host, I want to thank you for all you've done . . . for me."

The Beast's heart is pumping, (can't you hear it?) In his gruff voice, louder than even the pounding of his heart, he asks, "Would you like to come in, sit down?"

She nods, smiles.

They walk into the firelight-soaked den. Ophelia takes it all in like Cinderella at the Ball. The Beast gestures towards his large reading chair. Ophelia curtsies again and sits in the chair; she resembles a child-Queen on the throne of an adult-King.

The Beast sits cross-legged beside her, resting his large arms on his even larger legs. Their eyes and faces are on the same level and they stare at each other, wordlessly, until the Beast is forced to look away, at the window, then at the dress, the white, dry, clean, dress. He'd washed it himself, to get the smell of river and seaweed off it, then hung it to dry for weeks in the hot basement. It shrunk a little, but was still beautiful, half-transparent like a wedding dress.

Finally, the Beast stutters and then says, "I . . . I didn't *know*." He looks her in the eye. "I'm sorry."

Ophelia turns away from him. Her fingers trace patterns on her dress, H and A and M shapes. "You acted out of the kindness of your heart. For that reason, you are a good... soul." She traces an L up her thigh. "You found a dead girl and brought her back to life." Quickly, cursive-like she draws an E and then stops. Her entire body freezes. "How were you supposed to know she wanted to die?"

Silence. Thunderclap, in the distance.

"And now," says the Beast, "do you still want to die?"

"No," she says, followed by a pause. "Not that I want to live either... but I do *not* want to go back *there*. Not yet anyway." She wipes a tear from her cheek.

"My Hamlet is dead, killed by my brother. I don't know if I can ever recover." She looks up at the Beast, a hopeful glint in hopeless eyes. "You have magic... Magic to resurrect the dead. Do you have a spell to make me forget this pain? A healing spell for the heart?"

The Beast shakes his head, ponders his own body for a moment, and says, "There are some things even magic can't cure."

✻

Like a broken heart, he should have said. Or grief. Or shattered faith.

Ophelia *never* recovered. But she stayed with the Beast and they lived happily, like cousins, or close friends, for the rest of her life.

Forty-two years and four months after drowning herself, Ophelia died, again, of natural causes, in her bed, in a black dress. When the Beast found her the next day, the sheets, the dress, and Ophelia herself were soaking wet.

A Beauty, Sleeping

Imagine this:

A framework of red roses, with red stems, twined together like red-faced lovers. Vertically aligned beds of chrysanthemums and lilacs and American beauties in the background; a Pollock of reds and whites and yellows. In the foreground, on a star field-sprinkled sheet, a glass case, like a huge block of ice caught in time. And inside, a woman, a beauty, sleeping. Sheathed like a mummy (*sans* head) in white satin pulled taut over her narrow body, stretch-pant-style. Layer after layer in a latticework pattern reminiscent of East Asian quilt-paintings. Above her shoulders, she was free of it. Her long, shining, golden hair reached her pelvis in her horizontal state. It was curly and therefore wavy: an ocean for her face to swim in. Pretty features, in any century, locked in juvenile radiance. With her eyes closed, her mouth trapped in a somnambulant scowl, she looked sad.

✽

Stepping back, you realize there are lights around the "set." Huge, expensive-looking contraptions on metal stands, supported by sandbags, leaking wires, creating shadows where before there were none, lighting the glass coffin from four different directions. Crew wander around with bundles of wire on their shoulders or hang out next to the craft service table and guffaw.

The photographer circles Beauty like a jungle predator toying with wounded prey. He snaps shots quick and violently: a junkie, shooting up. *More, more, more, more* . . . Then, he stops. There's a *snap* and an angry sigh; the roll ends. The photographer, European, gay, well-dressed, shouts, "OUT!" as loud as he can.

Beauty is oblivious.

*

In actuality, she is *old*. Ancient, actually. They found her in the seventies, in some corner of the Scottish mountains, nestled between a T-Rex fossil and half a Mammoth. It took only a few days before they carbon-dated her glass coffin: Centuries old, from a time before Grimm or Anderson or even Straparola.
The Real McCoy. The original. The inspiration.

*

"She's a legend, alright," says a roadie near the set. He leans against one of the studio's massive walls. "You know how many people she's made millionaires? *Billion*aires? I'm talkin' journalists, photographers, lecturers, filmmakers, talk show hosts. Actresses playing *her* in the story of her life. There's a musical version in New York, updated with all the facts, of course. Whole companies, Advertising corps., jewelry makers!, banking on her, putting her ads and on products. You know what she is?" He smiles, takes a long drag off his cigarette, lets you ponder for a moment.
"She's a golden goose," he says. "*Money*."

*

She's been passed around like a high school whore on the first overnight trip of the year. Museums, talk shows, news magazines, art galleries, endless photographers and filmmakers, the occasional Millionaire's party, even widely advertised concert venue appearances.
COME SEE THE REAL SLEEPING BEAUTY!
Live at the Fillmore. Live at the MET. Not really alive, though.

*

It's not a very interesting show.
First, there's the history lesson. "Once upon a time, in a kingdom far far away, there was a young princess . . ." Then, the dramatic unveiling. The lights go dim, the drum rolls begin, then, curtains of

various dark hews of purple reveal Beauty, herself. The glass case, now on a velvet couch and inside, the star of the show, silent as a corpse.

There are multiple cameras on her and tight shots of her face fill up dozens of screens around the stage. Blonde hair everywhere.

Finally, the upclose viewing, a precession of bodies like at a funeral, come to give final respects. Again, it's nothing too extraordinary. She looks the same up close as she did in the countless photos in the countless magazines you've got at home.

Maybe you're hoping she'll wake up, just then, just for you, (lucky you). But then you remember she's dead. She's a million years old. She has to be dead.

Right?

✸

The photographer shouts again, this time for a cigarette. "Cigarettaaaa!" he shrieks. Some young kid wakes up from a nap and then rushes forward, pulling something from his back pocket and tripping on a loose cable.

Thousand-dollar lights buckle and shake and start to fall. A *crash*, and a lightning-flash of electricity ignites the long black sheet. A fire flares up around the red roses, the painted stems, the wall of color.

People are shouting. Sparks and sudden flares appear everywhere. Rage-filled flames surround Beauty's glass case, a funeral pyre worthy of a legend.

The photographer, suddenly chivalrous, attempts a run at Beauty, to try to save her or . . . something. His crew holds him back, wrestles him outside. They shout curses at each other or at you or at God.

✸

Whose fault was it, then?

✸

Nighttime.

Fire trucks are lined up in two columns, half a dozen, spraying their multi-colored lights, a drug-induced-CGI-Technicolor-dream.

The crew stands apart from a mob of journalists behind barricades. The press is inexplicably silent.

The moment lasts a long time. Then, slowly, firemen start to file out of the still-smoking studio, their eyes downcast, their shoulders slumped.

The European photographer, a ball of anxious energy, runs up to one of them.

"Well?" he shouts between pants. "What. Happened. To. *Her?*"

The fireman nearest him pauses, looks up. There are slashes of red on his face. (Paint? or . . .) The thousands of shards of glass on the cement floor reflect the lights on his yellow uniform back into his face. "Dead," he says, barely audible over the sound of flames. "She's dead. Cut-up when the glass exploded."

"Wait!" someone, maybe you, shouts from the huddle of journalists. "You mean, she was alive? Until . . . *this?* And no one bothered to check . . . all this time?"

Another endless, empty moment. No one answers.

Then, someone in the crowd, a young man in a suit-and-tie, wipes a tear from his lip and whispers, "That would have ruined it."

Rapunzel Goes Mad

Her name was Llewellyn.

An ornamental name for an ornamental girl, strange syllables and random consonants, stretching, hanging, like her useless limbs. A stump ended her right arm in a period, a broken-jointed-knee on her left leg (comma-shaped), and a missing eye, always covered by a patch; her most guarded deformity. She came from a small family with a small farm, hidden in the woods. She lived in the barn, with the horses, and was rarely seen.

Her name was Llewellyn. A pretty name for a pretty lady. Out of loneliness, she grew out her raven hair until it looked like the fluffy tails of the steers. So long they called her Rapunzel. So long it covered her arms and even went far enough down to hide her misshapen knee. She covered her missing eye with a swash of it, like a textured brushstroke on canvas. She practiced her walk until she got it right, wore a tiny brace on her knee, and a girdle to keep her back straight. She brushed her hair a thousand times each day.

At nineteen, she moved to The City. Nineteenth century New York City, rife and alive. She bought a penthouse apartment in the East Village.

Her parents gave her their savings; glad to be rid of her. Enough to buy lavish dresses and attend upscale Park Ave. parties. She was a rarity: an unescorted women, her hair like a flock of furs around her.

When introducing herself (for men were attracted to the mystery of the long-haired-lady), she said, simply, "Llewellyn." She had no last name. No family, no fortune. Yet, still, they courted her. During a gorgeous (and sometimes dreadful) Indian summer, she was the talk of the town. They waited to hear her secrets, revealed.

But she denied all her suitors. She would never allow anyone (no man nor woman) to see her true nature, to see through the hair to the truth. She took no lovers, no husbands, and no friends.

So, as the cool winds blew into the emptying streets, they stopped talking about her. She was regaled to the easy category of the female outsider, for which there are many names: "witch," "crow," "dyke," "hag," etc. And in keeping with the role, she aged quickly, badly. Cut off from the sun and the rest of the humanity, she lived alone in her high castle.

Maybe she was waiting for a prince. . .

She stopped cutting her hair and so it grew and grew and grew until it filled every inch of her tiny apartment. Walking around was like navigating a thick downpour. She often had to stretch an arm out in front of her or she'd hit a wall, or a chair. She lived a life of utter quiet, surrounded by strands of darkness.

Maybe she was happy. . .

Eventually, Llewellyn woke up from her decades-long-nap. She *pushed* aside clumps of hair, like coagulated dough, and looked at herself in a mirror. An old woman, half an arm, one leg shorter than the other, one eye missing. She laughed. She laughed at herself.

A wild, animal air about her, she ran out of her apartment, naked, trailing her masses of hair like a thousand tied together wedding dress trains. She escaped her building onto moonlit streets, deserted. She roared, with a mixture of tears and uncontrollable laughter, "HERE I AM! THIS IS ME! MY NAME IS LLEWELLYN!"

One witness, recalling the sight the next day, reported seeing a "naked, crazy woman, raving, carrying a dozen quilts behind her."

"Most rude," said another, "she woke up half the neighborhood!"

One man, an older gentleman in a top hat and a neat black suit, called this writer over for a hushed conference. He said he recognized the woman, the endless Rapunzel-hair, from a long ago party.

He said, "Her name was Llewellyn."

Doll Parts

Across the street from the Shoes and the House of the Seven Dwarves lives the girl with the golden hair and her husband, Rump. They met in a fairytale. You know the one. There was a devilish monarch, a terrible marriage, and a magical affair. The King treated her like a slave, a peasant girl to be fed and fucked. They placed her in a room at the end of the darkest hall they had and made her work. They put a spinning wheel in her room and delivered beaten straw to her door with meals.

It was all too much for the sad brunette girl. She had been a Princess in her homeland. She was used to being pampered and protected. So, she cries. She cries all day and all night. Her tears fill the crevices in the stone floor until she's ankle-deep in water. The water steams as if warmed. A child-like image appears in the haze. When the smoke clears, an imp stands in the center of her room, looking around, grinning.

His skin is green, his eyes the color of sunflower petals. He is immaculately dressed in shades of purple, a top hat, and perfectly polished black shoes. When he sees her, he smiles.

"Ah," says the imp, "right on time."

"Are you here to free me?" the Princess asks in a little voice.

"Yes. But I ask for something in return."

"Take my first born!" she cries on cue.

The imp shakes his head. "I don't think so." He looks her up and down, his mouth curving into a sneer. She knows that wicked sneer from her husband.

It is short and dramatic much like the imp. The Princess is flustered afterwards. Her body tingles like after a run.

The imp nods at the spinning wheel. Suspicious, she moves to sit at the machine. She strings the straw into the rollers and begins to cycle with her feet. The brown, brittle, strands transform into a sparkling metallic yellow. In minutes, a hill of gold lights up the room in bright shades of orange.

The King is pleased.

The Princess pleads for her life. "You are now richer than ever! Grant me a divorce and let me go. Give me my freedom."

He doesn't look up from staring at his newfound fortune. "Do it again tonight and then I will grant you your freedom."

Later, he sends bucketfuls of straw to her room. The stacks touch the high ceiling. The Princess tries the trick again, but with no success. The imp appears. They fuck, this time longer than before, and then she gets to work. She finishes the stacks as the sun comes up.

Once again she asks for her freedom and once again the King says, "Tomorrow."

The episode is repeated night after night for days. Finally, after five nights of sex and labor, of hope and rejection, the Princess, exhausted, falls asleep at the loom. Her head topples forward and her hair slides into the machine. It pulls like an angry child yanks at a doll's hair. The pain is a blinding flash. Her hair, now bright and shining in a golden luster, is clumped on the floor.

Her scream wakes up the imp. He watches her fondle the hair and touch her naked scalp in disbelief. His little heart fills with pity (and some lust). He wrinkles his nose, waves his arms, and her hair floats above the floor and reattaches itself to her head. It spins around her scalp in a twirling merry-go-round of gold dust. And when it's over a beautiful blond-haired Princess shines like a mini-sun in that cramped little room.

She looks down at the imp and says, "What can I do to repay you?"

"Marry me," he says in his best Prince Charming voice.

And, of course, she agrees.

✱

The town is built on rocks. Look out any window, you won't see rolling hills and a bottomless blue sky, but black protrusions jutting out of the ground like misshapen genitalia. The ground is the color of mud. Houses are built in funky shapes around and in between boulders. Sidewalks zigzag to avoid particularly rocky patches. Roads curve dramatically like all good roads do.

Her house is covered in rain-stained stucco. The exterior is a dark shade of white. Inside, everything is papered in dust. The heavy blinds over the windows never open so the light inside is diffuse and sparse.

Despite what you might think, she cleans. She has a duster the size of her head and she runs it along every surface and object in the house. She spills a bucket full of soapy water on her kitchen floor and scrubs ferociously with a large mop. She polishes the mirrors, admiring her shiny hair and the smart lines of her face.

But it doesn't last. She returns to the living room. The dust is still there, a film of grey on every surface. It's as if a colorless ghost follows her around, staining everything in her wake. Its name would be Spite.

At lunchtime, she sits down at her kitchen table and pours herself a drink. Vodka looks like water. Tastes like death.

✹

She hates this place, hates the patchwork streets, the nostalgic houses, and the secretive, paranoid, people. She hates the way they look at her and Rump. Envious and violent and condescending and hungry all at the same time. Rump was the one who wanted to come here. He knew some people from back in the archetypal forest. They hooked him up with a job at a nearby doll factory, untangling piles of plastic arms and legs. Separated, he feeds them into a shoot and they get whisked away and re-combined in perfect form. He used to bring home the doll parts and give them to her to reassemble into whatever form she wanted.

Rump seems to be working more lately. If he's not at work, he's at home asleep, exhausted from the heat of the factory and the stress of keeping up the illusion of a normal life. Weekends are short, busy with needs—mostly sexual. When Rump goes to sleep early on a Saturday night, she goes out. Her impossibly blonde hair stands out wherever she goes and men find her. It isn't just her sex they crave, but the promise of energizing life in those hollow eyes. She meets Princes in back alleys and bathroom stalls and, for a while, it dulls her boredom.

Sometimes, though, her midnight liaisons don't go well. She finds herself in disgusting bachelor pads in bad neighborhoods or getting groped in dive bars. She escapes and finds her way to a diner on the one road up to her town. The diner is run by the Duck family.

The place is busy for the middle of the night. One of the Duck daughters, her white apron strained yellow with grease, recognizes her and ushers her to a booth in the back. She doesn't have to order. The girl goes into the kitchen and comes back out with a large chocolate shake. The metal tin is as full as the glass. She drinks it slowly, enjoying the thickness, the richness. Maybe it's the sugar or the alcohol, but she feels light-headed after a while.

After an hour or so, the diner thins out. One solitary customer, an old man reading a newspaper (today's? tomorrow's?), shares the place with her. The Duck daughters come to see her, a wave of scent, icky grease and tangy sweat, comes with them.

The three of them squeeze into the other side of the booth. Madeline, Maud, and Matilda. Two of them are heavy, wide and bulbous, the third a thin rail, sickly looking and pale. All of them have criminally unwashed hair, their skin is creased and saggy like old money, and their noses are long and flat. They are meek and they have trouble looking anyone in the eye. The matriarch of the family, a Killer Whale of a woman with a big mouth and wide rounded limbs, often berates them in front of customers.

"Hello," she says. It's all she can manage at the moment.

"Hey. Hi. Ho."

The middle one, Maud, raises her head and speaks up: "Tough night?"

She nods.

"Want another shake?"

She shakes her head.

The thin one—the quietest—sniffles and says what the whole town thinks, "You know . . . You should stop. You have a husband. It's not healthy."

She *hates* that everyone knows her business. She feels suddenly livid. She wants to get up and scream. But she doesn't. She looks at the girls. They attempt shy smiles at her.

If only they knew would it was like to be *her*. Then they'd see.

Rump's wife smoothes out her hair and stands up. "Come by the house tomorrow night," she tells them. "I have an idea."

❋

The Duck girls barely fit on the bed. They're all limbs and hair and noses.

Rump's wife is sitting on a rocking chair beside the bed she shares with her husband while the girls seem to take up all the air in the room. They're pretending they're at a sleepover in some teen-centric movie. They're doing each other's hair and talking about their futures, or lack thereof.

Maud, maudlin, says, "Everything would be so different if we weren't here."

Rump's wife nods and smiles. The Ducks hailed from a different place than the ancient forest Rump pulled her out of. They come from some shiny and bright Kingdom with anthropomorphized animals. The rumor is that the girls' parents had an incestuous affair and were banished to the real world by the mice and the dogs.

She tells them, "This place isn't so bad. There are so many things to do and see. You could be anything you want."

The girls share sad looks. The oldest, Madeline, says, "We don't know what we want."

The youngest, Matilda, looks brightly at Rump's Wife. "We want what you have." Here she almost stops but then continues. "We want excitement, passion."

Maud sums it up, "Sex. We want to have sex."

❋

The next morning, she goes to Rump for help. Usual for a weekend, he sits in his chair watching some game where men run around and chase a ball or the ball chases them, she's never sure. He cradles a white can on his belly. His whole body seems to be covered in a drowsy pallor.

She tells him of her plans for the Duck girls. "I want to help them like you helped me!" she says. "Free them from their prisons."

Rump is suspicious. What is his disloyal wife up to now? He knows, from experience, selflessness is not such a hoity-toity emotion, usually it is tinted with personal desire.

Rump throws up his hands. His can of beer tumbles to the floor, spills on the dirty carpet. "I don't have the magic anymore!" he says, suppressing a sniffle.

She moves closer to him, bending her body to fit the contours of the chair. She gives him a familiar sneer and runs a finger slowly up his thigh to his crotch. "Maybe we can find it again," she whispers in his ear.

He perks up. The drowsiness melts away, that easy. His little body seems to glow. His hand wanders onto her body. Where he touches her leg or her ass, she feels a pocket of warmth. Hungrily, he follows her up the stairs.

*

The girls make some incredible progress in strength and confidence. She teaches them manners and how to hold their heads up above the level of men. They turn the rock-strewn street into an obstacle course, jumping over hurdles like soldiers stepping through tires. They practice yoga on Rump's weedy front lawn. They put on makeup for the first time in their lives and quickly wash it off in disgust.

Finally ready, they go up to attic and unwrap the old spinning wheel. It came with them from the other world, somehow. It's become a nest of moths. She smacks the air around it with a broom until all the moths fly away. The former Princess, hesitating, sits down at the wheel, memories flooding her mind. She shakes her head and calls the first girl over. One by one, they are balded. Their frizzy black hair carpets the floor like barbershop debris.

She goes back down to see her husband. He is napping on their bed. Their room, like the house, is dark and dreary, dust-soaked. As they fuck, she catches his eyes in a mirror. They have a distant, distracted, sheen.

After, she goes back to the attic. The three bald girls are huddled in a corner. She sets to work on the spinning wheel, threading their sticky, rough, clumpy hair through the old rollers which squeak when they move. The flattened hair that comes out the other side isn't gold, the source was too malnourished for that brilliant shade, but it is bright and white and resembles bleached copper.

They assemble the hair together and use ties and pins to reattach it to its respective owner like wigs. They fuss with it, tilting it back and forth till it almost looks natural.

And then they are ready. The three bleached-blond-haired girls step out of Rump's house on a clear summer day like they'd never seen before. The sun reflects their hair and brightens the careful smidgens of color on their cheeks.

But there is no one there to greet them in the town. No applause and no midnight ball to go to. In fact, there are no "eligible bachelors" anywhere in their little world. What are their choices? The Shoe boys? They smell like sweat and dirty socks left on the floor for a week. The Beast's? They are more likely to howl at the moon than a girl. And the Dwarves? With their matching china, prissy outfits, and sing-a-longs, they are so obviously gay.

Who then? Where are the Princes?

They turn to Rump's wife. She had promised love and sex and adventure with her stories. Where are *her* Princes?

She turns away from their hateful looks. She can't bear to tell them the truth. Her "princes" are of the lowest kind available. They ride the highways on chariots of oil and rubber. They wear leather jackets that smell like cigarettes and cheap liquor. They are patrons at the Duck's diner. They are regular people.

And when she doesn't answer, the girls start crying and run home, tripping on rocks.

*

Their mother, of course, is in a tizzy. She waves her dough roller like a whip, threatening to smack them.

"*What* have you *done* to yourselves?" she screams. "You look like whores! Like that whore down the block." Her face scrunches up into a mean scowl. "*She* did this to you, didn't she? Speak up, brats! You want to be tramps like her? We'll *see* about that!"

Roller in hand, telephone in the other, Momma Duck spreads her poison through the town. She makes up all kinds of things. She says her daughters are out whoring themselves. She says Rump's wife is sleeping with her husband. She says Rump's wife is sleeping with *all* the husbands.

And by nightfall—these things often happen at night in these tales —a mob forms amongst the boulders: women in aprons, men with torches, small children there to "learn a lesson." They form a

cluster in front of Duck's Diner and then march towards Rump's house. When they arrive, angry and passionate, they start to shout:
"Come on out, hussie!"
"Face the reaper, girl!"
Etc, etc. But no one emerges. Not even Rump.

Inside the house, Rump's wife searches through the gathering dust and dirt and clutter. She kicks over drawers and cabinets in the rooms and capsizes couches and chairs all over the house. He's small, he could be hiding anywhere.

She holds a bottle of two dollar wine in one hand. Her blond hair looks like hay left out in the sun for weeks and her once pristine features sag as if she's aged a decade in a day.

As she surveys the house, a strand of her hair gets caught on a shoulder-height nail. She is so busy running around in her drunken haze, she doesn't notice it. Her hair slowly unspools. She crosses and crisscrosses the house, leaving thin tendrils behind in her wake. Finally, the last of her hair pops out.

She collapses. The shouts of her neighbors come filtered and ugly into the house. She cries. But nobody appears to help her this time.

He left her, finally. She should be hurt and angry, but she barely feels anything. Not even surprise.

Outside, the mob grows angrier by her brush-off of their big collective statement. Their screams and shouts get louder and louder and then suddenly hush as if someone pressed MUTE on a remote.

Rump's wife walks out onto the lawn, alone. The crowd doesn't recognize her at first. She wears an old nightgown. Her bald head shines in the moonlit night, her makeup black and smeared across her face. She doesn't look like a Princess. She looks nameless. She sighs, drops her bottle on the lawn, and studies the crowd.

Their stares bore into her in that quiet moment. She sees their desires in their eyes. Their souls are dancing and laughing at her. She wants to dance with them. She wants to be like them, on the other side, one of the gawking gawkers, not the subject of the story, but just a casual viewer.

One day, she'll have her chance.

Number One Hit

The highway is paved with the bodies of musicians. Their bones crunch under the weight of our motorcycles, a staccato of shattering and blistering bones, every once in a while a cleft-shaped sigh or a note or two of some long ago number one hit. The concentration of dead musicians is heavy here: lots of bleached hair, clown makeup, sequins, fake diamonds glinting in the fading light, and tattered venue posters, colorful and forgotten.

Not to us. We haven't forgotten. We're salvagers, musical pickers, historians with a good ear.

The front bike slows and so does the other five, wheezy engines and clattering brakes kicking up an ominous intro.

"Got something on the sensors," says Burr, up at the front. He lets one meaty paw off his handles and grabs his sensor doohickey to show me. As if I could read the tiny screen from my bike. As if he already knows I'm not going to trust him.

"I don't hear nothing," I say.

We all cut our engines, a song rudely interrupted mid-track, and listen. There's the wind, the tin of our bikes cooling down, and the far off cry of a person or animal dying.

Then I hear it. A guitar, just the faintest hint of twang, strings angling like a harp.

I look back at my people. As silent as we can, we get off our bikes and grab our weapons.

Burr, big beast of a man, points towards a collection of towers a few minutes walk from the highway. We get into a loose defensive formation and start towards it, two men staying behind with the bikes.

On the side of the road, away from the clutter of the highway, is only grey rock. Trees are of the dying or on-the-floor variety. As we get closer to the towers, the clutter underfoot resumes with pieces of ancient equipment: keyboards and mice, splintered cabling and even some old telephones. We try to avoid making noise. We want it to be quiet so we can hear if there's any-

There it is again. The guitar, this time accompanied by a beat. Just a classic Casio pre-reset but it's enough to get our spirits up. We give each other genuine smiles before continuing forward, our guns out.

"Watch for lurkers," I warn as we enter the area of shadows.

The towers are really server racks full of computers with criss-crossing multi-colored cables. Some are large like statues, others are half-destroyed and leaning like Pisa. The equipment within are in varying stages of destruction. Once this collection of computers ran the world or hosted some banking software or porn website, all the rows full of blinking green lights. Those lights have been out for decades now, the domain names long forgotten jokes ending with a dot NET or dot COM.

My crew stalks silent-like through the debris. The music is steady now, as if someone settled on the right station in a sea of static. I can hear vocals, a whispery female voice, sadness in the inflection.

Someone behind me releases a sharp intake of breath. It's Whizz, a long haired, long bearded, long legged dude who never shed a tear in his life. He looks away from me.

"Move!" I shout into the wind.

We all rush forward as if someone rang a dinner bell.

Behind one of the towers, huddled together for warmth, a group of three teenagers in rags stand around the glow of a monitor. One tries to run. Whizz tackles him to the ground.

It gets very noisy. One of the teenagers, a girl, starts crying. I'm shouting something about raising their hands. The one that tried to run is fighting back. Whizz is having fun, dodging punches and doing a little dance.

That soft guitar music is still going on from near that screen but I can't hear it.

"JUST SHOOT HIM!" I shout. Whizz shrugs, pulls out the smallest of his pistols, and shoots the kid in the face.

A sudden return to silence. Louder somehow than the music, thicker.

I look over at my techie, Gena, short with pink pixie hair and spikes around her neck, wrists, and ankles. She pushes aside the teenagers and sits in front of the screen. She slides her finger across the screen a few times.

"What we got?"

"Usual," she responds. "Kids must have found the one live port in this fucking toilet, hacked in and found a cache of MP3s in a backup."

"How many?"

She looks at me with a slight grin. "At least fifty... albums."

"Let me see." I scrunch down and watch the screen as she scrolls through. Lots of obscure trance shit from the 20's, some heavy techno, some pop. I stand up.

This is the first decent catch we've had in a while. I look around at the quiet world around us, the decaying towers, the electronic debris, and the music coming from the screen and decades ago. We won't be alone for long.

I look back at Gena. "Do a database search, see if you can find anything else hidden away. Copy to a flash and then destroy the tower. Quick now."

"Boss." Burr, big and hairy and smelling like sweat, is standing behind me. "We should go."

"We will."

"We can't be the only ones around."

I turn around to face him. He's tall and bulky, but so am I, with at least one hundred pounds on him. I get up into his face. "You got a problem?"

He takes a step back. Shakes his head. "No," he says then looks over at the teenagers. "What do you want do wit' them hackers?"

I walk over to them while Gena is inserting a skull-and-bones flash drive into a port on the side of the screen. One girl, one boy. They could be siblings, maybe even twins. All these techies look the same: white skin with a greenish tint, black glasses, some form of patchy jeans jacket and black-as-soot jeans. My eyes linger on the girl, her dark hair unwashed, skin full of pimples. She keeps her eyes on the ground but I admire her tits under her tight white shirt rising and falling with her tension.

I'm talking to Burr, but for their benefit. "We probably should just off 'em here, save us some trouble." They scrim a little, the boy especially is thinking of some escape. My guys got pistols at the back of their heads and they looking like they ain't had no fun for awhile. "But ... This is a pretty nice stash of music they found on some pencilpusher's hard drive. Could fetch some serious cash, assuming there's a NOH in there somewhere." I take a deep breath, exhale like a God. "We do owe them for that."

Burr is getting antsy, I can tell. He wants blood, I suppose.

I get down on my sizeable haunches. They're afraid to make eye contact. I reach out to the girl, who flinches at my touch, but I squeeze her chin just enough to get her to look at me. She's pretty for a vagabond. She's frightened, shaking, but in those green bespectacled eyes I see something lacking in my crew: intelligence.

I guess I'm feeling generous today.

"You kids need a job?"

*

There's the World Outside, dead, quiet, sad if you're prone to thinking too much, and then there's the World Inside, loud, crowded, smells like shit and piss yet preferable to the silence above.

We roll down the big dirt ramp into the underground city, my bike in the lead, destitutes crowding the road, carrying sacks of food or possibly family heirlooms. The masses scuttle aside for us, clutching their belongings and young girls. We set up the two hackers in a wagon side-hitched to my bike. They're holding each other tight and staring at everything with infant eyes.

I call out to them, "You never been down here before?" They shake their heads. I assume they speak, but I still haven't heard a word. "Whole life on the surface, huh?" I laugh. "You're missing the party."

At the bottom of the ramp, we round the corner onto the first flat street of the underground. The drumbeat is the first thing I hear. It seems to be coming from all directions. Syncopated to the rhythm of the city, the beats are ever present. *Boom, boom, boom!* Pedestrians, most covered in a brown dirt, shuffle from one open doorway to another. Hand-painted signs, like Grocer or Weapons, hang over every other doorway. Ladies in windows open their shutters and then close them again. A couple argues in hushed tones, their arm movements like a dance.

The sound of our bikes, so clear in the desert above, is lost in the din of everything around us. We ride slowly, our engines barely a whisper, towards the center of the city.

"This is all housing," I say, feeling the need to educate. I motion to the one or two story mudbrick buildings. "Not much to look at, but these structures can hold dozens of people. They sleep twenty or thirty to a room. It smells bad, but it's safe." As we get closer, the streets get thinner and the sounds more erratic. No longer the steady beating heart of a city, but instead the occasional shriek or heavy breathing, a window slammed closed, or a muffled scream of a baby or a dog.

"We're getting close to the Hub now." I can see it through the break in the small buildings. The tallest structure in this quote-unquote City, a piecemeal hovel that somehow stretches five or six stories high, made of a latticework pattern of different building materials, the center of all roads and commerce in this place. We don't go any closer than we need to.

I slow down in front of a small building, some walls actual brick, most just ash-colored clay. Above the door, a printed sign in a flowery font reads, *Wanderers.*

The place brings a white smile to my black heart. Inside it's straight out of a make-believe fantasy inn. Big wooden bar at the back with animal heads hanging from the rafters. Tables full of gruff-looking sonofabitchs huddled over steel pitchers, planning and gossiping. Gena goes straight to the barkeep to make arrangements. Some of my guys see long lost friends and disappear into the corners.

Burr and the kids stay with me near the entrance. The eyes of the patrons are on me. I let them soak me in forawhile. Finally, I move towards a nearby table. Two sad sacks are sharing a single ale. I wait, wordlessly, until they scuffle away and I move in to claim a seat at the table. It's a good table with a view of the front door and the bar. I nod at the two hackers and they sit down across from me.

Burr, full of nervous energy, is still standing behind me. "Boss," he says. I ignore him. "Boss!" he says, again, loud. "It's been too long, boss."

"Fine!" I say, throwing a hand up. "Have fun."

He walks over to the otherside of the table and whispers something to the hacker girl. Then he pulls one of his huge arms around her chest and lifts her up. She tries to struggles, her 90ish pounds against Burr's two hundred plus and fails very quickly. She looks at me for help.

"Calm down, baby," I tell her with a wink. "You may enjoy it."

The boy moves to stand up. I stare at him. "Sit. Down." He does, as Burr throws the girl over his shoulder and walks towards the back of the bar, upstairs to the rooms. "Don't worry," I tell the kid, "he's not going to hurt her." I can't help but smile. "Well, not that much."

Gena comes to the table, carrying some drinks. "Arrangements made, boss," she says. "We got the whole top floor."

"Perfect!" I say, grabbing for one of the steel mugs. At the top is a brown foam, a good sign. I take a long deep drink, finishing at least half of the cup. It's good beer, fresh. Gena grins and walks away.

The kid is staring at me, his eyes like fire.

"Don't be such a fucking prude," I tell him, finishing my first drink. I reach for another. "Is she your girlfriend?"

"No," he says.

"So what's the problem?"

He doesn't have an answer. I smile, buzzing. I ask him, "You have a name or should I make one up for you?"

"Tim," he deadpans.

I laugh and tighten an imaginary necktie. "Tim. Serious name for a serious guy. How old are you, Timmy?"

"Seventeen."

A little bit of compassion fills me. "Ah. Born post-Crash. You have no idea about what the world used to be like."

"I've seen pictures."

"Hmmpf! I'm sure you have." I look away at the sad faces of the other people in this place. "You have no idea what we've lost." Inspired, I reach into my jacket, into one of the many crudely stitched inner-pockets and pull out a worn paperback. Its pages are yellow with age, the cover is secured with scotch tape. It's an English-language version of *One Hundred Years of Solititude*.

"Do you see this book?" I ask the kid. "Do you know how many people, all over the world, have read this book? Could you even imagine a number so high? Millions of people, in hundreds of languages, all across this planet, have read this book. There will never be another book like this ever again. It's like the music we salvage. It's special because it's a kind of extinct species."

"But," says Timmy, suddenly brave, "People can still write. People can still make music."

"Yes. But no one does. Not for a long time."

✱

Later, I stumble my way up the creaky wooden stairs to the top floor. It's late and I'm vaguely aware that I may be waking up the building with my drunken footsteps, but I don't really care.

Up at the top floor, in the shadows at the end of the hall, Whirr stands up, nods to me. He's "on watch", making sure no thieves come by our rooms, but his cheeks are red and his eyes a bit more cloudy than usual. He's been drinking. I should be upset, but I'm not.

I walk to the only room with an open door. My bags, a half dozen tattered shells that usually hang on my bike, are set up carefully on a desk. I rummage through them, through yellow newspapers and bullet casings and tar-smelling clothes, until I find an ancient cassette player. It's just a black box, scratched up like crazy, but it means everything to me. I rummage again, this time pulling out small in-ear headphones that were once white, now dirty beige. I go into my bags again, shoving my hands in the stickiest corners of the bags, until I pull out two small cylinders. I push open a slot on the back of the player with my thumb and insert the batteries into the player one at a time.

Exhausted by the search, I fall into the tired structure this place calls a bed. It seems to be made of straw and wood, but it's more comfortable than bare rock, which I know from painful experience. I clutch the box in my hand. Slowly, I reach into my jacket and grab a scratched up cassette, a souvenir from one of my first raids, and place it carefully into the player. I put the headphones in my ears and close my eyes.

Music fills my world. I feel like I can touch it.

✱

The next day; and my head hurts like a bitch.

I drink two cups of coffee downstairs before going back up to fetch my gear. By nightfall, we'll be out of this town and onto the next one. That's always the plan.

My guys get their bikes loaded up and ready in an alley beside the Wanderers Inn. Timmy and the hacker girl stay close together. She looks tired.

Gena, Whirr, and Burr surround me as I load up my bike. They're full of questions.

"Who's goin'?"

"What ya takin'?

"Canicome, Boss?"

See, the Hub is like an exclusive club from back when society was segmented by class. Only certain people can enter the Hub and they can bring only one or two guests. It keeps the riff-raff out and the goingson behind the doors a mystery to the normal people. Every underground city has a Hub and they're all connected through whats left of the world's Internet.

That last part is kind-of a secret. Most people think the Internet's been dead since the crash. People better off that way, my opinion.

I've taken each of my Top Three to different Hubs throughout our journeys, but I'm still feeling generous. I silence the three of them with a look and say, "I'm taking the newbies."

"What?!" they shout as one and follow up with some choice expletives about me and my mother and something about a dog.

I smile at them and walk over to the kids.

"Timmy," I say. He straightens up, looks at me with those small frightened eyes. The girl, whose name I learn is Emma, looks at the floor. "You and the girl are with me."

They share an infectious smile.

"Good!" I say, slapping my hand on a nearby wall. "This will be fun!"

They follow me back to my bike. I feel the need to educate these two, to spread my hard-earned knowledge on non-knuckleheads like my usual crew. They position themselves into the cab and I jump on my bike, revving the engine to get it going. The Hub casts no shadow in this subterranean world, but I can feel its pull from here.

On the short ride over, I'm quiet. My sudden need to pontificate is replaced by the danger and dread of our destination.

The guards at the gate raise their hands in greeting. They're wearing helmets with dark visors that obscure their features. They've each got pistols on their hips and the two guards nearest the door look to be carrying pulse rifles.

"Business?" inquires the nearest guard.

"Music," I reply in the typical shortclip of these situations.

"Cred," he commands while the other guards keep their hands near their pistols.

I pull out a small lacquered card, bequeathed to me by a dead former colleague, it still smells faintly of blood and gas, and show it to the guard. He nods and his minions relax.

"Off," Mr. One Word intones.

I shut down the bike and nod at the kids to step out of the cab. The guards move in closer, some raising their guns up at us, the others with old-fashioned metal detectors. At every beep, Mr. One Word reaches into my clothes and pulls out a gun or a knife. One hand comes very close to the crack of my ass.

"Careful there, buddy. Nothing goes in there."

I smirk at him and then look over at the kids. The guards are padding them down and they look disappointed when they don't find anything.

Mr. One Word appears to be tired of us and breaks his usual routine to spit out a *sentence*. "You'll get all your weapons back when your business is concluded."

The doors start to open with a loud crunching squealing sound. One Word continues his screed about decorum and business practices while in the Hub but I stop listening. I rev the engine and pull forward into the Hub.

The first room is a garage/anthechamber. There's small clusters of people huddled around cheap tables. Motorcycles and small cars line the walls. I pull into an empty space and nod at the kids to get out.

"Stay close," I tell them.

Near the elevators, there's boards filled with chalk scribblings. Only some of it makes sense to me, certain acronyms highlighted in my mind's eye, a small pond of sanity in an insane display. There's five elevator banks but each one only goes to certain floors. By following the lines of chalk from the letters NOH's to a floor number, I see we need to go the fourth floor, second section.

I stare at the roman numerals over the elevators. Emma brushes past me, "This way," she says.

I almost protest, but realize a second later she's heading in the right direction. I give her a long stare while waiting for the next car to arrive. She shrugs at me. "I like codes," she says.

The elevator door opens and a dozen people step out, some smiling, some downtrodden. Twice that amount of people, myself included, push ourselves into the large steel box. It's cramped and the air is thin. Emma and Timmy are right up against my belly, they have to bend their backs to fit in the space. When the elevator lurches upwards, the lights flicker and threaten to die, but don't.

After a short ride, the door opens again. Inside the heart of the Hub, it's like a Vegas Casino from the world that was. There's activity everywhere, lights and sounds and smells. Girls in tight bodices walk around smiling at strangers, guys in suits that show their muscles move slowly about the crowds, and hanging from the ceiling, screens full of fast-moving codes and numbers, a stock ticker for antiques. This is the most active and colorful of all the Hubs I've been too. It's like a party, where everybody is toasting the past. A funeral.

Every few feet is a large oval-shaped table with four or five screens spaced judiciously apart. In the center of the oval, a stern looking individual squints at the figures behind the screens: Overseers. They're the judges of the deals, they decide what's fair or not and finish off the deal. They always take 10%.

Emma and Timmy are frozen in place, wide-eyed like children.

"Come on," I tell them, pushing past them. "This way."

Each oval is themed in a certain way. Some trade in movies, those ancient forms of entertainment that seemed to fill up most people's lives, some trade in TV, the equivalent of food for the previous generations, they gobbled up hours of the stuff every day. But the most exclusive ovals, those that interest me the most, deal in music. Music is the sound of nature as translated by the human experience, it has no equal.

The music oval is off near the edge of the massive floor. The mass of the crowds is thinner here, although it's still a little too busy for my tastes. I sit at an unoccupied screen, the hacker kids hanging out behind me, scoping out the area like they're my bodyguards. I pull the skull and bones stick from my jacket and insert it into one of the many hidden ports behind the screen.

The Overseer walks over to me. They all look so much alike, it may be a robot, but it seems like a man with a thick Texan accent. "Buying or selling?" he asks.

"Selling."

He nods, presses a hidden key, and walks away.

On the screen, the list of the newly acquired songs scrolls by on the right side. The system checks file names versus data, verifying things like sound quality and legitimacy of titles. Slowly, numbers appear by the song titles, going-rates of songs by that artist or time period or genre on the global exchange.

This is the waiting phase. My cache is being submitted to hundreds if not thousands of other consoles in other Hubs or the personal screens of rich collectors in the few remaining cities in nicer parts of the world. Near one of the titles, a small red exclamation point appears. The system has flagged the song has an NOH. Once, for a brief moment in time, this song was the Number One Hit of a world that no longer exists. Instantly, bids start to come in.

I start clicking through them, as fast as I can, ignoring everything except the top price, which keeps rising. I hear a grumble beside me. I look away from my work. Emma is staring at me with an angry look.

"You think you can do this better than me?" I challenge her.

"I *know* I can."

I stare at her eyes. That hungry knowledge is still back there, despite whatever my boy Burr did to her last night.

"Fine," I say and give her my chair.

She sits down with a flourish and starts sliding her fingers across the screen like a pianist doing Mozart. Another red exclamation point appears near another song and Emma is already combo-ing that piece with the first one. The big number at the top of the screen, my possible profit, keeps jumping by hundreds of dollars. She's ignoring the top bidders and pushing the middle-ground bids to drive up the demand. Other songs, not with exclamation points, but by the same artists are suddenly in the triple digits.

If there was music in this place, I'd start dancing.

I glance at the Overseer, who seems very interested in Emma. He's hovering near her, one eye on her and one on his secret screen.

Passerby's pause when they see the girl with the magic fingers. A few linger. I shove a few out of the way while blocking the view of others. I don't like attention and the girl is gathering some. Even the other bidders in the oval are glancing up from their screens to peer curiously in her direction.

Then I see the number at the top of her screen. More money than I've ever seen in my life. Somehow she's taken two NOH's and a handful of obscure shit and turned into a major score. I feel my dick getting hard and my breath tightening up. I feel proud of my decision to bring the kids to the Hub and amazed to my foresight not to kill them in the fields.

The Overseer, perhaps tiring of Emma's cleavage or the sudden crowd, chimes in: "Final bids are in. Sell or leave."

Emma looks back at me. She's also breathing hard, sweat pooling around her temples and dripping down below her cheeks.

I smile at her. "Let it ride, baby!"

She slaps the screen, a big red icon that says **SELL** in bold. There's a bit of cheer that comes from the crowd. Even the Overseer cracks a smile.

"Your winnings are on the way," he says, that accent morphing 'winnings' to 'waaaanings'. A couple of suit muscleheads walk over with a thick white envelope.

Giddy, we walk away from the table. The kids are chatting about the bidding process, the tech and the thrill of it. My brain is riding a million miles an hour. With this much cash, my crew can stop roaming the wilderness for antiques. We can settle down somewhere, start a local operation, start a family again, be normal. The possibilities are endless. I smile wide as I think about sharing the good news with Burr and the others.

Emma, Timmy, and I wait for the elevator. Emma tugs at my arm. "We did okay?" she asks, sheepish grin on her pretty face.

"Better than okay," I say as the doors open. I let the kids in first so I can hold on the envelope in front of me. I'm aware of others looking at me. The elevator quickly fills up.

There's a lurch as it gets moving and then another as it stops and the lights go out, this time all the way. I feel the knife enter my back and I'm about to yell when a hand clutches my open mouth.

"Scream," Emma says, her breath hot in my ear, "And I push it all the way in."

The pain is intense, like a volcano inside me. It seems to quickly spread to my arms, which feel useless, and my legs, which buckle. I can feel Timmy, thin and quick, slink to my front in the dark and grab the envelope.

"No," I whisper as the knife goes in further.

The elevator kicks back into operation and the lights flicker on. Somehow, Emma is front of me, her body pushing me against the wall. There's a laugh from someone else in the elevator.

I can taste blood in my mouth. I can't move or speak.

The elevator stops and the crowd pushes its way out the doors. Emma leans in to me like she's going in for a kiss. "Thanks for everything . . . *baby.*"

Before my vision disappears, I see her and Timmy rushing out towards my bike. Some dark figures appear over me. There's some shouting and the report of guns firing.

When the darkness comes, it's like nothing I've ever heard before.

Do What You Desire

I saw the stars and I cried. I'd never seen them before.

Centered on a canvas bordered with branches and leaves, they shone like bullet holes in black paper, too numerous and bright to be real.

I'm used to the city. The mega-cities that once were states. I was born and raised in the city of California, one of the largest in the world. The mountains to the east and the water to the west buffer the city; a burn-mark across half the coast, dark as scorched earth during the day, alive as a sparkling disco-ball at night.

My parents always warned me against leaving the city. "Daniel," they'd say, "stay away from the country, it'll swallow you up. There's nothing there. Blank space between here and somewhere else." They never said anything about the stars. They had no idea.

Try to see the stars in the city and all you'll get in return is the piss-color-yellow of light pollution. Look up. There's nothing there. An absence. An absence of stars. The light of the city negates them, scares them away. Maybe that's why cities feel so lonely.

Back in the country, the everywhere-stars embraced me in their warm, white, everywhere-light. Like holy light but without the holes.

I could see my reflection up there. Connect-the-dots: It's me. It's me walking, alone. Then other figures, other shapes, quivered into life as if out of nothing. I recalled their names like long lost friends. The figures moved, danced, played, slowly, as methodical and mechanical as an automaton. An archer pulled back his bow. A knight-on-his-steed galloped forward. Orion grabbed the Big Dipper into his hand, scooped up the brightest star, and ate it.

Then he looked down at me.

And I shivered.

Words appeared now, formed from the negative space, bright stars next to not so bright stars. Letters and nonsensical sentences, random and strange like fortune-cookie-fortunes or high-school-paper horoscopes.

Do what you desire.
This is a glorious beginning.
GET OUT OF THE CITY.
The stars spoke and I obeyed.

*

First, I went to Canada. I figured north = closer to the stars. There was still wilderness in Canada.

I bought supplies. Suitcases full of books; a telescope; maps of the universe, I taped them to the ceiling of my car.

Hilltops work best, I've discovered. Not mountains. Mountains are like the Tower of Babylon; sacred, dangerous. *Too close.* The stars would not approve.

Down at the bottom of the hill, I could see my car, silent, enjoying a well-earned sleep while I sat in a hard-backed chair with loud Scottish music playing on headphones, my telescope set up beside me, scattered books at my feet like dirty clothes on a dorm room floor. A woolen fleece and, of course, strong coffee.

The stars woke then, as if they felt the caffeine coursing through me, and began to percolate. I tossed the coffee aside, scorching some nearby grass, and stood. Staring straight up, I twirled about like a child in a House-of-Mirrors. No images this time, but long slashes of white against the darkness. Words coming slowly like someone just learning how to spell.

The stars said, **Go East.**

*

So I did.

Toronto: the size of a province, where I had to drive for five hours just to get to a decent lookout-point. Cities were the only places I could find jobs. And it wasn't just me.

Urbanization had spread like The Plague. Highways went from congested to deserted, as more and more millions of people escaped the heat and pollution of the "wide open spaces" to huddle together for warmth and comfort in the shade. Cities now resembled a floor full of upright dominos, tall building after tall building, at roughly the same height, pushed up right next to each other. The city, more so now than ever, had become pure shadow.

New York City: like the open eye of a whale, the brightest and largest of the dots of light, a city the size of pre-secession-Texas. I stayed at the edges of it, worked temp jobs in downtown office buildings (all of them covered with massive black UV-protection sheets), and drove out to what once was the Midwest to see my stars.

I kept my nights free, always. I made no friends and those I once had, I lost contact with; or they lost contact with me, I can't remember. I stared at the stars every night (weather permitting), yet they denied me.

I told myself I stayed in the cities for the jobs, for the money: for batteries, for food. But I'm a liar. I'm a cityboy, accustomed to nameless strangers shoving me, getting in my way, waiting in line behind, being afraid of. Bothered by. Cuddled by (every once in a while).

The stars had singled me out, separated me from the multitude, *chosen* me. But now . . . were they upset? Angry at me?

The thought strangled me in my sleep.

So. One shadowy afternoon, I packed as much of my belongings into my car as I could and drove out of the city, heading south.

*

To the coast of Florida and a sailboat.

As the sun set in a marriage of blues and oranges and fire reds, I set out, on a boat as white as a tooth, with a single sail and a tiny motor. It took me far enough.

The stars were unshackled above the ocean. They posed and pranced about just to see their reflections.

Hopeful, I reached out like an infant, trying to touch the untouchable, but they never let me have them. The stars were chaste.

*

And silent. For years!

Rejected, I felt like a broken button, or a light switch connected to nothing: useless.

I almost gave it up.
Burning inside, I told myself, *if they've denied me, I will deny them.* I won't be their bitch-puppy, muzzled and house-broken, playing nice in hopes of getting a treat. I stood up on the rocking-chair-like-boat and shouted my rage at them.
"Fuck me? No, fuck *you!*"
Grief-stricken, I immediately apologized and begged for their forgiveness.

*

I went away again.
I smuggled myself, hidden like the Trojan horse in a crate, from Atlanta to the European Coast.
I had a thousand dollars and a backpack.
I left most of myself in America. Novels I had loved since childhood, worn photographs of my family, my car/best friend, favorite TV shows, favorite foods. Things that had, somehow, glued themselves to me as I crisscrossed the continent for the past two decades.
I'd become an old man without my consent. Years of little sleep and minimum-wage-labor had carved lines and crevices in my skin. A cragged cigar-smoker's face at thirty, a sunken-eyed cancer patient's at thirty-five, a bum's grime and grub-filled skin at forty.
I was not as timeless as my stars. I *showed* my age.
Crouching, hidden and freezing, in the bowels of the ship, I told myself, *This is going to be good for me.* A new beginning. Just what I needed.
Then I went up a deck and scavenged the trash for food.

*

Lisbon, Portugal.
Immediately, I got as far away from the Eastern European Metropolises as I could, hopped trains, northwards, till I hit water and chilly Norway.
Snow settled on every inch of ground, house, tree, and bush. Sometimes the temperature dipped below twenty, Celsius.

I longed for my car and its sunroof. I learned hiking and cross-country skiing. But the travels were tough and slow-going. It took half the night to trek up a nearby mountain just to sit and stare for less than an hour and then rush back before frostbite had me bedridden.

I took up drinking. Just for the warmth (really). I went out with my books, my maps, and a thermos full of Vodka: The Russian-Blood-Warmer.

And it worked. No more biweekly colds and bedrest. I could keep up a consistent vigil, stay out for whole nights if I wanted too. At work, the next day, answering phones and gophering from desk to desk, my movements and reaction times were sluggish. My mind was distant, heaven-bound. Occasionally, gentle coworkers would ask me out to join them for dinner or dancing or drinking, but I'd decline. I was always, always, busy.

I spent a year and a half in Northern Europe without a word or gesture from *them*. Maybe it was a language problem?

✱

I left again. I continued east, towards the Middle East, by way of Turkey.

Some desert-heat would be a welcome change of pace, I told myself.

I settled, this time, in Israel, on a Kibbutz in The Negev: a wide, triangle-shaped slab of desert separating Israel from Saudi-Jordan to the east, and Cairo to the west. The Kibbutz was a self-sufficient community, every resident was expected to work for their food and lodgings.

It was perfect for me. I no longer worried about my dwindling cash or finding sheds or abandoned farms to sleep in. I had a small apartment with no kitchen and two rooms. A job tilling and seeding. Three meals a day. I even kicked my vodka-habit.

To see the stars, I only had to walk for ten, fifteen minutes, into the shrub-farms surrounding the Kibbutz.

Look up. There they are: calm and peaceful in the wilderness, in the joyous *lack* of humanity. No one for them to be afraid of here, so they smiled at me. Forms of light, resembling a woman, then a man, embraced, spilled milk merging on black linoleum, and twirled across the night sky, like Beauty and the Beast.

I dreamed up an imaginary woman to sit with me.

Unfortunately, it wasn't long before I drew attention in the small community. In a city, you'd be fortunate (or unfortunate) to know everyone's name in your building. Even that was unheard of. But here my strange sleeping patterns and distant and anti-social personality drew me out into the open: a news-item. A topic of conversation.

The people were polite in their concern. They never spoke to me directly, and since I never initiated conversations, I never spoke. They secretly peeked out their windows at night and watched me tiptoe through the thin cobbled streets. In daylight, they whispered to each other as I passed.

I saw them, some nights, stepping out of their homes in the dark, looking up, straight up, just like I do. Hoping to see something unique instead of just the stars. (They took them for granted.) Maybe they were hoping for a comet or a spaceship, but they weren't patient enough. Stay out there for a few hours, a few days, then, maybe, if you're lucky, you'll get something to talk about. Or keep to yourself like the comfort of a secret.

The stars, maybe sensing the increased eyes, remained silent.

Finally, the people of the Kibbutz, politely, but *en masse*, asked me to leave. When I asked "why," because I knew they would be honest, they said, "You're scaring us."

✱

Your parents probably told you, "Don't stare at the sun, you'll go blind."

They never said, "Don't stare at the stars, you'll go crazy."

But they should have.

✱

I wandered Asia for an indecipherable amount of time. Cloudy time. Hazy time.

The people I met were mostly country folk, kind to an old traveler, not prodding with endless questions. They didn't want to know all the sad stories of all the sad wanderers in this sad world.

Sometimes, though, they *would* ask me. Badger me with parental-sounding questions, like: "Who are you?" "What are you doing?" "Where did you come from?"

They could see the mark of the stars on me. I indulged them. I whispered things about a "quest," a "mission," a "destiny" and a life-long-adventure.

Lies, of course.

But adventures were so rare these days.

*

Once, I tried telling the truth.

I was a little drunk and a little curious. Would they believe me? Pity me? Or just laugh?

I was in Thailand at the time. A village of mud-colored wood huts and dark, warm, people. They were used to strangers. People came to this country to get away from everything else. The mainland was sparsely civilized while the coast was dotted with a long trail of lonely dots, like a sleeping serpent's tail.

The people were warm and friendly. They took me in. When they first saw me, trudging up the beach from some rundown train station a few miles away, I had my backpack slung over my thin shoulders, my clothes ripped, grayed, and filthy and I reeked of garbage, oil, and sand.

The villagers lent me a small hut. It had a real mattress, child-sized, with embroidered blankets and pillows, with American hotel insignia. I slept, curled in a fetal position, for thirty-six hours straight. Then they fed me: jasmine rice and little strips of chicken, seasoned with peanuts. They gave me American-brand razors and a bottle of shaving cream. I used them gladly. They were the kindest people I'd met in the whole world.

Later, sitting with them around a campfire, drinking mug after mug of a strong beer-like-brew, lulled by the heat and hospitality, I began to talk. My voice was hoarse and rough, dust growing like mold in my mouth over the years. But I gave it my best shot and spoke slowly. One of the teenagers, a boy of eighteen or nineteen who worked as a waiter at one of the hotels, was my translator.

"One night, I saw the stars, for the first time in my life, and I cried." The boy whispered the translation, the language shooting forth extremely fast like machine-gun-bursts. "I was just . . . happy to be witness to something huge, bigger and better than me. But then, as if they *knew*, they woke from their astronomical sleep. They *spoke* to me."

Whispers from the audience; shared looks of doubt. I answered their looks with a steady stream of truth. "No loud, booming voice. No burning bush. But simple words. They told me to go, to leave my life, and to follow them.

"I don't know why. I don't know why they chose me. All I know is I . . . I had to listen. My purpose in life became clear, perfectly clear like water, and there was no more doubt. There was no more questioning who I am. I knew exactly what I had to do."

I paused for a few long minutes. The boy, and the crowd, looked up.

"I've sacrificed everything I had. I have nothing left to give up. I've wandered in search of answers for a lifetime. Sometimes, though, I wish it would stop."

Night-silence. The crackling of the campfire.

One of the old men in the audience, face and body shadowed in rags, whispered some machine-gun-words to the boy, who looked at me with a smile.

He spoke in a very accented, floral, English. "You can stay here."

I didn't know what to say.

"You can stop."

"I . . . I would be honored."

I looked up then, at the static stars. It had been so long since they spoke to me, I had forgotten their voice. They didn't move. They didn't talk. They didn't inspire.

"Yes. Yes, I accept."

I was so happy, I cried.

✸

Later that night, I went out to say goodbye to my stars.

(I know. I shouldn't have. But I did.)

They blazed as if burning. Phosphorescent brilliance. Faces appeared, scratched onto the night sky as if in chalk. Appearing, then disappearing, quick, like an Etch-a-Sketch. Me. And me. And me again.

My faces. Me at twenty; at thirty; at forty; at fifty, progressively darker and scarier. Like a ripple in a lake, the images shimmered and were replaced by a sentence. Wide columns of lights for each letter: a boldface.

It's not over yet.

I stayed in the village another day, enjoying the food, the warmth, and the shy smiles from the women. The next night, I sneaked out while they slept, heading north, to find a plane or a boat to take me eastward.

Back home.

*

To America, and the massive California Colony, recently seceded from The States.

The city was darker than I remembered.

No traffic whizzed past on the streets. No cars lined up beside the pavement. No overflowing restaurants, bars, or clubs. There were darkened windows showing empty businesses. I looked in, hopeful for even a hint of other humans, but saw nothing. Starless-sky-nothing.

Look up. To see a dull sheen of blue behind semi-transparent black. The city, fed up with blocking out the night, now focused on the day. Cancelled it out.

I wandered the empty city like a character in a science fiction nightmare. I shouted, but it only echoed back at me, again and again, bouncing off the buildings, like clothes trapped in a dryer.

What happened? I wondered. Where *is* everybody? Even lost in the global mess of time-zones, I would have heard of something like this. A nuclear scare? A mass exodus? A war?

I walked down streets with recognizable names. Sutter. Rodeo. San Francisco. Streets that stretched like highways, from the border of Mexico-City to what-once-was Oregon (now part of the city of Sealand). I walked and walked. The dim day became black night. And, above, shining now, my stars.

I stopped, and stood, dumbfounded. The stars were moving, racing, actually. More images than my eye could see on a canvas the size of the Heavens.

Charged, I ran into one of the abandoned buildings. Leaped three-stairs-at-a-time, until I reached the door to the roof. There I hesitated. My body was tingling, an incoming rush. Like when you're about to get too drunk but you're well, well, on your way and there's nothing you can do to stop. So you close your eyes and hope for the best.

I opened the door, stepped out into the chilled night air. The stars wrestled with each other. A laser-light-show complete with distant music. I glanced around . . .

And that's when I saw them, the others. *Congregations* of stargazers, fifty to a hundred per pack, standing on every other rooftop for as far as I could see. A few of the rooftops whispered music. The people stood as if in rapt attention, their necks craned all the way back (it hurt to even see), eyes and mouth wide open, inhaling the stars. They looked like zombies at a car-less drive-in.

And that's when I noticed the words. At a close level to the rooftops, a snaking river of words, like a news-ticker at the bottom of a television screen. The phrases were similar to the general, but seeming personal, fortunes and inspirational phrases the stars had first greeted me with. But upgraded. The phrases had names attached, like songs dedications over the radio.

Dennis, you will find happiness soon.

Kelly, you are right. He is wrong.

Rachel, caring comes before passion. Be patient.

It took me a few minutes to process. The names were like graffiti painted on the walls inside my brain.

The stars were not just talking to me.

And that's when my reality went supernova.

I fell to my knees, beaten. Clutched my heart in case it fell and broke, like everything else. Like my childhood, my past, and my future.

I closed my eyes, but they wouldn't stay closed. The city continued its silent worship. Something about the ease of the others as they watched the stars had a gasoline-like effect on my anger. The way they just stood there! They didn't need to discover anything, adventure anywhere. Like sheep!

I felt, in the tumult of conflicting emotions inside me, cuckolded.

I took off my overstuffed backpack, huge and ugly and over fifty years old, and let it drop like a stone onto the rooftop. It broke, ripped, and spilled. Decaying books and coffee-stained-maps of the solar system, obsolete now. DVD-discs: Archaic pieces of technology. Souvenirs of a wasted life. I picked up everything I could and threw it over the side, rushing about like a love-crazed teenager, or a man possessed, until there was nothing left. People in nearby rooftops watched me from the corner of their eyes.

I thought about suicide.

But then, a familiar image, not a face or a horse or an archer, but a name, a name as lost as my youth: My name, another fragment of the past from someone else's life. The name was connected to a phrase, caught in the river, circling about me like a stubborn mote of dust.

Daniel, you are special. You were the first.

My mind raced.

"Did I fail you? Why did you abandon *me*?"

The stars sounded remorseful. **We didn't. We were protecting you.**

"From what?" I shouted.

From this.

I looked away, then. Down below, I saw darkly-dressed men and women streaming out of buildings and scattering, a dreary, wasted, look to their movements. Faint sounds of car engines and distant vendors. That *ting* of a bell from an old door, in an old Mom-&-Pop. The smell of hotdogs. Cigarettes. Dogshit.

City sounds. City smells. They all came flooding back as if, somewhere, a dam broke.

And that's when I realized the city was not dead or abandoned, just sleeping. The city had actually stopped. For the stars. For my stars.

✱

It's like, when you were a child, coming home smelling like alcohol or cigarettes, and your parents berated you with cliché after cliché after cliché; like, "If everyone else jumped off a bridge, would you, too?"

Yes, Mom, I would. I'd jump first.

The Conductor Sighs

"I'm not feeling very inspired these days," I tell the orchestra.

They respond with the unique sounds of their instruments. Thankfully, I speak music.

"But why?" they say with a blare of horns and a twinkle of woodwinds. "Look around you! There's war." A bassoon roars. "There's famine." Screeching of violin. "There's suffering." A somber clarinet.

I sigh. "There's too much!" I pierce the air with a flourish. The response is a barrage of sound, a discordant mess of pain.

"Use it!" they say. "Use your tears. Use your anger. Use it all."

I shut it down with a sword slice.

"No!" I shout. "It's not mine to use. I'm not suffering. I'm not starving. I'm not dying."

A thin metal rod hits a triangle, the sound is massive, it echoes around the hall, the city, the world.

"Not yet."

*

Walking home that night, the cars and trucks compose a concerto. I cringe from the sound. Mechanicals are always complaining.

Most of my fellow passengers on these rain-slicked streets have earbuds in their ears. I envy their ability to pick and choose their own personal soundtrack.

I need to get home. My wife and son are waiting. It's past his bedtime but I know they're awake. Even if I only get to see him for a few minutes, it's worth it. I kiss his cheek, I sing him a song. He tells me an anecdote or two from his day. It's the kind of quick exchange that's become normal in this hyper-busy time. "Quality time" as a clip, a tweet, a short.

I'm almost to my block when I hear a trombone call my name. I stop. A door to a jazz club is open for a few seconds to let in some patrons. When the door closes, the sound is cut off mid-syllable and I rush to it.

I open the door to the club and enter.

There's a background beat, a story told in grooves and toe taps, there's a heartbroken saxophone and that slow-motion moan of a deftly played trombone. It's silky smooth. It's medium rare filet mignon. Béarnaise on the side.

My son is waiting but I sit and order a drink.

The band is two older black guys and a horn-rimmed white dude on the younger side. They're telling stories of, what else, lost love. Floating on the surface of their arrangements, I can see a wispy brunette at a picnic and a shy boy. They're young. There's a lake nearby. They kiss under the night sky.

The music turns sour.

Now they're older, living in a shitty apartment uptown. They work a lot. They fight. They regret things. There's no happy ending.

The songs ends and there's a moment of utter silence, followed by a long round of applause. Smiles from the musicians.

My beer is only half done but I get up and go.

I glance at my wrist. Fuck.

✽

My wife doesn't say anything when I come into our apartment. She's watching TV.

"I'm sorry," I tell her. "He was okay?"

"Yeah, sure."

She's pissed. Tired, too. Mostly tired. I'll be here tomorrow evening, I assure her. She knows I'm lying. Afternoon and evening rehearsals are common in my line of work.

We watch the news for awhile. The latest war, the talking heads with their terrible agendas. It doesn't inspire. It makes me numb.

After some time, she signals forgiveness for my offense by curling up beside me. She rests her head on my shoulder and I can hear heart and her pulse, whispering to me. They are comforting sounds, past sounds. When the snoring starts, I slink away and put a pillow under her head and cover her with a blanket. I lower the volume on the TV but don't turn it off.

At the far end of our apartment, we have a little office nook in a corner flanked by two windows. I shift my wife's laptop aside and bring up some musical paper scribbled with notes. I tear off the top sheet, throw it away.

I think of the state of the world my son will grow up in. I wonder if my own father thought the same thirty years ago. Was he as scared as I am now?

Use it, they said.

I sigh and look back at my wife. The fact that I know her so well makes me feel warm inside, content. I remember when we first started dating. There was a picnic too.

It was a hot summer day so we found a shaded area between boulders and trees. We had those sealed cups of wine and deli meats and cheese. If I close my eyes, I can hear the birds conversing on the wind, the background murmur of the city, and the reassuring sound of her beating heart.

I start writing a couple of upbeat positive notes to kick off the composition. I can see the shape of the piece of my head, the penumbra of emotion, the bright highs and the inevitable lows. It won't always be bright, but it doesn't have to be.

Time Keep

There is a tiny town at the tip of time. Think of time as a pyramid. At the bottom are the ancient eras of dinosaurs, massive oceans, and century long winters. As the pyramid narrows, the eras are shorter and busier with life. And balanced at the top is a town full of tiny people. Though the town has no official designation, you may call it Time Keep.

The Keep's mayor, a bulbous man, well-coiffed and dressed primarily in navy blue, is named Mr. Sturges. Eternally a bachelor, he lives in the top most floor of City Hall. Every morning, he drinks his tea and stares out the circular window to the town square and the clock tower that serves as a replacement sun. The face of the clock is shaped like a pyramid.

The past few decades have been very busy in the town. Once every generation, the pyramid is flipped and time resets itself. Floods and massive storms blanket the planet called Earth, which is the single purvey of the Keep. The clock is rewound and time starts anew. Time moves differently in the Keep so one generation up here accounts for thousands of years below.

The Mayor rises from his chair and picks up his pocket watch. It is a gold-plated disc with the names of all previous mayors etched into it. His father's name is the last on the list and then his grandfather and so on through his ancestry. Sturges has no children. When his time in office is up, the townsfolk will hold their first election in centuries.

Or so they think.

He descends the spiral staircase to the third floor of City Hall where his assistant hands him a type-written schedule for the day. Her name is Mrs. Point, a bookish be-speckled woman in a beige dress.

The mayor peruses the schedule. It has the usual meetings with Management. It has an hour-long block of time in grey with no label or description. Sturges smiles at Mrs. Point, folds the paper schedule neatly into his pocket, and proceeds downstairs.

The rest of the morning is dull, as usual. Sturges half-listens to petitioners with minor grievances and cabinet members with their endless agendas. His mind wanders to the grey area of his schedule. He stands up and checks his pocket watch.

"I need to go," he announces, "or I'll be late." There is some protest, but it is half-hearted.

Mrs. Point is waiting for him at the large wooden door downstairs. Sturges puts on his coat, a slightly darker shade of his signature blue, his bowler hat, and grips his favorite walking stick. He thanks her then steps out into the morning. The Keep has no sun or moon or day or night yet the town was built to mirror the Earth below it so it has morning time and night time and the sky lightens and darkens through some trickery. He's never been quite sure of the specifics, except that it works.

He steps onto the cobblestone streets of the town square. He stops at a few of the open-air carts, businessmen and women selling fruit and other perishables, and chats with them while they offer him gratis goods. Every passerby nods at him.

The townsfolk are, for the most part, hard-working stalwarts of the way things have always been. They don't question their work, deep in the bowels of the town with the large gears and the heavy machinery of time. But there are others who spend hours sitting at the edges, gazing below to follow the brief lives of the Earth people.

It takes him a long while to wind his way out of the square. He enters a deserted alley and then surveys the street. When he's satisfied that he's out of view, he ducks into an vestibule and to a small door, half concealed behind a garbage bin. He knocks three times.

A small, dirty, man opens the door. The superintendent of the building is a short and fat fellow. They always are. He leads the mayor without a word through his darkened apartment and to a dingy elevator.

He's already excited. This is the part he loves the most. The clandestine maneuvers, the danger of being caught, exposed. There's a noise from down the hall. He freezes as if that would make him invisible. When the noise dies down, he continues to the furthest door down the hall and knocks once.

    The dark-haired woman who opens the door is naked. She's been waiting. He grabs her waist as he shoves the door closed behind him, much louder than he should have. He feels that danger reverberate through his chest and down to his hard genitals. His breathe is already coming out short and tight. He pulls the woman, whose name he can never remember (Linda? Beverly?), to a nearby couch and unzips his pants.

    It's quick, but satisfying.

*

Below the streets and the shops and the buildings of the town are the Gears. There are no days off and no vacations. Time never stops.

    One of the most seasoned veterans of the Gears is a slender and tall man named Mr. Benjamin Benedict. In the cavern that marks the entrance, tired workers, their clothes and skin caked in soot, nap between shifts on the muddy ground. In the rafters above the entrance are the latest examples made by Management. The shapes barely resemble that of bodies. They were hung there and starved to death.

    Benedict tries not to look up at the hanging forms. He follows the phalanx of people as they move closer together into the tight halls and dark passageways of the Gears. Wood planks cover the rock below. Steam shoots out from cracks in the walls and crevasses in the ground. Lanterns hang from the ceilings and sway with the occasional wind. Men shout to be heard over the clatter.

    He can start to hear the great force of the Gears while still on the elevator. He pulls two bright orange plugs out of his pocket and shoves them into his ears, making sure they are as far in as possible. The elevator continues its slow descent. The glow of the gold gears replaces the darkness of the topmost levels. Finally, the elevator stops and Benedict steps onto the metal passageways.

    He's worked here on Gold level for the past decade in a managerial position. Most of his day-to-day work involves scheduling shifts, but his passion is in the measurements and calculations of time. He's not considered Management, those people don't work in the Gears. They work in comfortable offices aboveground with their shades drawn. Ben files reports to them once a week though he doubts they are ever read.

He begins his usual walk around the various hanging platforms above the gears when rough hands grab him by the shirt and shove him into shadow.

"Hey!" he shouts. A hand grips his mouth to shut him up. He spins around to face his attacker only to see his brother, Charles.

"No time to explain!" Charlie shouts into his ear. He grabs Ben's arm and leads him down the hall and to a door he has never been in before.

Charlie ushers him into the dark room and shuts the door. The ever-present sound of the gears is muffled back here so they can talk without shouting.

"What is going on?" Ben demands.

Charlie is breathing heavy as if he's been running. They used to be mistaken for twins. He's shorter than Ben, but has the same lanky build and hair color. Ben keeps his sandy brown hair tightly-cropped, Charlie wears it long and loose. Ben never married, Charlie has a wife and two sons.

Charlie rummages around in the darkness for a moment. A lantern clicks to life and Charlie holds it up, illuminating the room.

In the center of the small room a rotund man is strapped to a chair. His arms and legs are tied with silver tape and his head is obscured by a hood, loose enough so that he can breathe. Ben recognizes the Mayor's distinctive form. Aghast, he looks at his brother.

"I screwed up," Charlie admits.

✹

The hood is made of a dry stringy material that keeps getting stuck in the mayor's mouth. He's tried to cough it out, but that's only made it worse.

Sturges can hear men whispering in the room. He knows they're in the Gears, in one of the deep levels. He can hear the constant churning and feel the reverberations in his chest.

Everything had happened so fast. After his brief but exciting liaison, he descended the elevator, still a bit out of breathe. The basement apartment was darker than he remembered but he still walked in like a fool. The men (or maybe it was just one) came at him from behind with a club or a hammer. He hit the ground hard and blacked out. When he came to, he was being dragged through the Gears.

He knows he has to try something. Despite the wooly texture filling his mouth, he tries to speak.

"Hello friends," he says from the inside of the hood. "If I may say something?"

A pause in the whispering. Sturges takes this as good sign and speaks up.

"Things have obviously gotten out of control here. Let's talk. Face to, uh, face. I promise not to rush to judgment or anger. We can make a deal, right?"

Struges smiles underneath the hood, hoping his conciliatory mood would be infectious. There's silence for a moment and then the sound of a door closing.

*

Above, news of the Mayor's disappearance has trickled out to the population. Citizens have gathered in the town square. Normally this is the time the square empties out, all the carts are wheeled aside and only young lovers and old couples stroll hand-in-hand, welcoming the evening. Tonight, there is a bevy of activity in City Hall. People rush in and out and whenever the wooden door opens, everyone tries to get a glimpse of what's going on inside.

The black suits of Management appear from one of the nearby buildings and stand like a lone black cloud away from the mass of people. They don't enter City Hall. They don't usually interfere with inter-town politics or goings on. Their focus is on Time. Still, the disappearance has obviously slowed work in the Gears otherwise they wouldn't have bothered to show up.

As the sky darkens, more people fill the square. Some of the clever cart owners start selling food and drink. There's an almost party-like atmosphere.

Finally, after the streetlights have been lit and the children escorted home, the large wooden door of City Hall opens. The Constable, a stern barrel-chested man with a thick mustache that shudders when he speaks, emerges. The murmuring of the townsfolk quiets. The Constable balls his fists and proclaims:

"We will hunt down whoever is responsible for this kidnapping!" His voice rises. "And we will make them pay!"

*

Ben and Charlie stand in a conspiratorial huddle outside the room.

Charlie has his hands up in a pleading gesture. "Ben, he was fucking my wife! I had to do something."

Ben shakes his head. "They'll hang you for this." He turns to walk away. "I'm not getting involved."

"Wait. Slow down!" Charlie grabs his brother's shoulder. "Maybe there's a way we can use this to our advantage? I know I was stupid and I made a rash decision, but maybe we can use this for the cause. We can-

"Keep your voice down!"

Charlie tries to keep his voice to a whisper just above the ever-present sound of the Gears. "Ben, we've been waiting for something like this."

"No!" Ben is rarely angry. "We can't be rash or quick to action. Not this time."

Charlie grits his teeth. The heavy sound of multiple footsteps comes from down the hall. The brothers share a frightened look.

This time, it's Ben who grabs his brother by the shoulders and whispers in his ear, "Go!" he commands. "Hide! I'll hold them off." He speaks fast, his mind racing. "When they're gone, go to my office. Under my desk is a hidden panel. You'll find a plan in there. Now go!"

With all his might, Ben shoves Charlie into the shadows.

The Constable's men rush into the hall and grab Ben before he can protest. They push him up against a wall. They open the unmarked door and when they see the bound form of the Mayor, they smile. Then their smiles turn dark and they set upon Ben, punching and kicking him until he goes limp.

Two of the deputies carry Ben back towards the elevators while the remaining ones untie the Mayor, apologizing all the while.

*

It's an event.

Morning in the Keep is usually filled with the steady march of worker's feet and the humdrum sounds of merchants setting up shop. Today, after a restless night for most of the population, the only sound is the rhythmic beating of a single tool in the town square.

A man is building a small stage and raising a long post in the center of the square. The Gears will be manned by a skeleton crew today. Schools will be closed. The decrees came out in the early morning hours in the long night.

In the Mayor's chambers in City Hall, Ben is tied to a chair in the center of the room. There are representatives from Management, the Constable's office, and many members of the Mayor's staff swarming the room. Ben's right eye is a mess of dried blood and more of the red stuff leaks out of his mouth.

"Look at him!" shouts the Mayor to the room. "He looks like a mess. We can't very well put him on display like this."

The Constable bows his head. "I apologize. My men got overzealous."

The Mayor throws his arms in the air. "Obviously! What should we do?"

"Perhaps a hood?" says the Constable.

"Let them see," says a scratchy voice. One of the representatives from Management, his words, like his face, caked in shadow. "Let them see what happens if they resist."

"Alright," says the Mayor with a mischievous grin. "Let's put on a show."

*

Down in the Gears, Charlie slinks into Ben's empty office. He keeps the lights off and rushes to the desk. He crouches down to the floor and reaches under the bottom of the desk to find some loose paper hidden in an alcove. He pulls the paper out and scrutinizes it in the thin light.

The first few pages are all equations. Charlie has worked in the Gears his whole life, but he never had the knack for it like Ben. He flips past the equations to a diagram. He recognizes the golden gears. He doesn't understand all of it, not even close, but enough. It will have to be enough.

*

Ben almost fell asleep before they slapped him awake and dragged up out of the chair. Strong arms carried him through the doors of City Hall and out into the square.

The air felt good on his open wounds. Then he opened his eyes and saw the whole town assembled. There were gasps from the women when they saw his bloody face. He shrugged off the men that carried him and planted himself on his two feet. Slowly, he made his way to the center of the square and the stage and the post that awaited him.

Ben always felt affection for the Earth people. They were innocent, like children. He had hoped to help them in some way before his time in this world was up. He failed, but he was not going to let that failure show, especially now in front of the whole town.

He held his head high as the Mayor and Management appeared. The mustached Constable emerged from City Hall last, his face grim and determined. He held in his hands some papers. When he got close to Ben, he nodded at his men and a noose appeared out of nowhere.

The Constable cleared his throat, looked down at his paper, and launched into a speech. Ben didn't listen.

*

"There!" shouts Charlie. "And there!"

He points at a series of gears. His men, or actually Ben's men, run to various edges of the platforms hanging high over the loud crunch of the gears.

Down here, loyalty is everything. If there is an accident, a mistake, any type of situation that might cause an injury, these men knew Benedict would be the first one there and ready to help. Now, he needs their help. Now is their time.

"NOW!" he shouts.

*

It starts with a rumble and then the whole square shifts as if the ground itself is angry at them.

People shout and fall to the floor. The Constable stops his speech. Ben smiles. He looks to the Mayor, who is white as snow.

There is another rumble, this time stronger and the wooden post and the noose connected to it fall to the cobblestones. Something erupts nearby. It's huge and gold. A gear lodges itself into the ground like a sculpture, then another one. They spit out of the underground in joyful rebellion.

The townsfolk scatter. Buildings begin to crumble and collapse.

Ben stands up. At some point in the confusion, Sturges had fallen to the ground. Ben extends a hand and helps him stand up. The Mayor is staring at the clock tower above the square. Ben follows his gaze and it lands on the pyramid shaped clock. The pyramid is spinning wildly as if reality itself was unmoored.

The Mayor has tears in his eyes. "What happens n-now?" he stammers. "To-to time?"

"I don't know," Ben says with a smile. And then he shrugs and disappears into the smoke and fire and confusion.

Maybe now they'll have a chance.

It Only Rains At Night

I stared at the flower for weeks. It was an upright twig in the beginning. Beige arms spouted and the trunk grew so thin and tall, it almost fell over. I wanted to help it, to reach out and hold it towards the sun until it could stand on its own, but I didn't. I couldn't. Its body was a penumbra, bent in sadness. As I watched over the course of a few days, it righted itself and dark green leaves were born off the strong arms. And from its head, a crimson flower blossomed into life.

The flower spent its short life dancing with the wind and drinking the rain. I never saw it rain. When I was outside, it was always the most perfect weather. In the morning when I came outside everything was wet with dew. Small pools of water napped on the leaves and the low wooden fence that was the border of my yard.

Over time, the magnificent magenta of my flower's early days began to wither and darken. I knew its time was running out. The green leaves on its body turned yellow and fell. I thought, if I could pluck the flower, take it inside, put it in a vase or give it a nourishing balm, I could save it.

The flower was located just outside the wooden fence that separated my yard with the World Outside. That's how my mom and dad always called it: The World Outside. Always with the capital letters as if their height might scare me.

It was only a few feet away. I thought, maybe I could just grab it and retreat? Maybe it wasn't such a big deal.

I looked back at the house. I knew no one was there, but I checked anyway. I placed both of my hands on the wooden fence and pulled myself up.

The sound was loud and oppressive like heat. It was a kind of buzzing but so quick it shocked me. It seemed to come from inside me somewhere or maybe it was just everywhere and it echoed most inside my chest.

I fell back into the yard. Dirt flew up and obscured my vision for a moment.

From the house, the voice of the caretaker, "Charlotte!" it called. "Are you alright?"

I coughed a few times. "Yes, I'm fine."

"What were you doing?"

"Nothing," I said. I stood up and slapped my dress with my palms to kick off the dust. "It was an accident."

The caretaker's voice wasn't coming from any particular place. It echoed around the yard like the voice of God. "Do be careful, dear," it said in its most endearing voice. "Come inside now. It's time for lunch."

I looked back at my flower. The magenta circle had brown on the edges that I never noticed before. The color seemed to have faded in the last few minutes. I knew it wouldn't survive.

✱

When I was very young, my mom and dad would tuck me in every night. Sometimes I wouldn't see them all day, but they would show up at bedtime. The caretaker dimmed the lights to my room and I would wait for them in the dark.

Sometimes they opened the door slowly, letting in splashes of light from the hall. Mom would sit on the edge of the bed and Dad would stand with his hand on her shoulder. She'd lean in so close, I could smell her apple-scented shampoo. She'd whisper, "Sweetie, honey, are you awake?"

Sometimes they were obviously in a rush and threw open the door, letting in an ocean of light. During these times, I would feign sleep. I knew they didn't have time to read to me or tuck me in. I was a good daughter. I tried to predict their needs and match my behavior.

They were always busy. Dad worked in a firm downtown and Mom oversaw a half dozen charities. Even when they were home, sequestered in their offices on two different sides of the house, I wouldn't bother them. I asked the caretaker to prepare breakfast. I picked orange roses from the yard and placed them in a tall cup on the tray next to the plate. I brought the trays into their offices as quietly as I could. They would be on the phone or typing on their computer. I'd leave it on their desk, smile, and walk away.

I've always been good.

As I got older, the bedtime visits lessened. They still sometimes visited to tuck me in, but never together. I'd ask Mom, "Where's daddy?" and she'd say, "Working." Or I'd ask Dad, "Where's mommy?" and he'd say, "Sleeping."

And then, one night, neither came to tuck me in. I stared at the door thinking it must be malfunctioning. I thought about asking the caretaker, but decided to wait another few minutes and then another. On and on until daylight.

Finally, I got out of bed and reached for the door. It opened without trouble.

The house was quiet and still. I walked through the halls adorned with paintings of my grandparents and great-grandparents and stopped at every door. I opened the doors just a crack and peered in. No one else was here with me.

I touched a panel on a nearby wall. "Caretaker," I said to the air, "Where are my parents?"

The cheery voice of the house replied from the panel, "They had to leave on an emergency issue yesterday. They should be back shortly. Would you like me to make you breakfast?"

"Sure," I said. I ran a hand through my unbrushed hair and headed back to my room.

The house said, "Please choose from the following options: French Toast, Pancakes, Waffles, Eggs Option 1—Overeasy, Eggs Option 2—Scrambled, Eggs . . ."

✸

I spent most of my days in the White Room. I called it that because that was its original form. Like the way you may still call an adult dog a puppy because it was once that.

When I first entered the room, it was like stepping into a cloud. The size and dimensions of the room were skewered by an endless white landscape. Only a small black square near the door called for attention.

School was held in the room every morning. The caretaker would manifest itself in the form of a globe with legs (geography), a tall giraffe wearing a librarian outfit (biology) or some other kind of caricature. After a long and dull morning, a faraway bell rang in slow lethargic clangs indicating the end of a session.

After lunch, I had the freedom to do or explore whatever I wanted.

The caretaker asked me, "Where would you like to go today, Charlotte?"

It was always the same. I said to the caretaker, "Mom and dad, please. Winter."

The white walls fell away to reveal someplace familiar. The grand living room on the first floor of my house. Snow was visible through the windows. A fire burned in the old stone fireplace. Large ornate chairs faced the fire. I sat down on the carpet in front of the chairs where constructs of my parents sat and drank tea.

I liked to pretend to talk to them together. Even though I hadn't seen either of them in a long time, it made me happy to think of my early childhood. I asked them the same thing I always did.

"Mommy. Daddy. When are you coming home?"

They shared a sad look. My mother said, "Soon, honey. The situation is volatile. Politically." She nodded to me as if that one word should say everything.

I asked, "Can I come to you?"

My father shook his head. "No, dear. It's not safe. You are safest within the house, under the protection of your caretaker."

I fought the urge to cry. I wasn't a child anymore. I needed to be strong.

"When can I leave the house?" I asked.

"Soon," they said. But I didn't believe them.

I fought back the tears as the bells clanged.

*

My bedroom was pink. When I was young, I loved pink. I wore pink dresses and all my dolls had to have pink in them somewhere, either pink hair or pink clothes. The last day I saw my mom, I was past my pink phase and so she had bought me a new dress. It was yellow with black dots. I called it my sunflower dress and it was my favorite thing to wear.

When I wasn't in the white room or sleeping in my bedroom, I was in the yard. I loved the yard even though it wasn't very big, but it was enough to keep me busy. I talked to the plants and trees, sang them songs about growing up and getting strong. When I saw a plant open and unfurl a stalk of seeds, I picked the seeds one by one and dug holes for them around the yard. I watched as those seedlings became sprouts then plants then trees. My life moved at the pace of plants.

There was a paved path running through the yard in a long S-shape. Using different colored chalk, I drew patterns and made up games. I always kept some chunks of chalk in the wide front pocket of my sunflower dress.

One day, while fiddling with a new plant that wouldn't stand straight, there was a great rumbling underground. I'd never felt anything like it before. The stalwart trees around me shook and it felt like the ground lost its texture, like it could swallow me up.

The caretaker called, "Charlotte! Come inside!"

I was frozen in fear. Aberrations in my daily life were so out of the ordinary that this new experience startled me to the core. I couldn't move at all.

The caretaker called again, repeating my name over and over until it stopped mid-syllable.

The world became dark. The bright clear sky of day fell away. I looked up to see a sky full of red clouds. Around me was the lush green yard that I knew so well but beyond the low wooden fence was more darkness. What was usually an endless landscape of green pastures and trees was a barren wasteland. I could see the wrecks of houses and trees reduced to stumps. The ground looked like an ugly shade of brown I'd never seen before. The air stung my lungs and I felt suddenly winded. I closed my eyes and slowed my breathing until it returned to normal, although it still felt hard to breathe.

I opened my eyes and my strength came back to me. I was able to move my legs and I, through nothing but instinct, moved towards the wooden fence and the unknown world beyond.

I realized, too late, that this could be my chance. As soon as I picked up my pace, the world lit up again. The blue skies returned and the world beyond the fence became the picturesque landscape I knew so well.

I didn't stop. Though my lungs burned, I ran towards the fence with the intention of jumping it without touching it.

The caretaker called out: "Charlotte! Stop!"
I ran and then jumped—
Into an invisible wall. I fell back, the wind knocked out of me. This hurt so much more than the buzzing noise. I put a hand to my face and felt the beginnings of a bruise on my cheek. I tried to get up but my back screamed at me to stop.

"I'm hurt," I whispered.

There was another rumbling, but this time it came from the house accompanied by a mechanical whirring sound like a motor. Two metal arms attached to long cylinders emerged from the ground near the house and picked me up. The cold fingers slid under me and lifted me. It hurt, but I didn't scream. I cried as the caretaker pulled me back into the house.

*

I knew every inch of the property. I knew where the paint was peeling on the doorframe in the downstairs bedroom. I knew there was something stuck behind the fan in the second floor bathroom because it rattled when it was turned on. I knew exactly where the border of the yard wouldn't let me go any further. I knew everything except how the caretaker worked.

It was a computer, I knew that. Computers need hardware. Where that hardware was located, I didn't know.

In the living room, there were bookcases set into the wall near the fireplace. I took the books down and tried to read them when I was younger, but the pages were glued together and the cover and spine were faded. I often sat near the empty fireplace and thought about my parents. Now, I sat down cross-legged and tried to figure out the caretaker.

There was a slight breeze I never noticed before coming from the fireplace. When I looked closer, I saw a thin sliver of light peeking out of the break. I ducked down and stepped into the fireplace. I ran my hand near the sliver and felt the wall. It didn't feel coarse like brick but smooth like plaster.

The caretaker's voice startled me. "Charlotte. What are you doing?"

"I, uh, I thought I heard someone call my name."

"There is no one there. Please return to your room."

I didn't listen. I pressed both hands against the back wall of the fireplace and pushed.

The false wall fanned open revealing a staircase into darkness. The air inside was stale. I descended a wooden staircase and found a switch to a single light bulb in the low ceiling.

The walls were exposed cinderblock and there was nothing but storage here, dozens of boxes with labels like "Living Room" or "Nursery." The room wasn't large. There had to be more. I checked the walls for more hidden passageways and searched through the boxes for any hints, but found nothing.

When I went back upstairs, the caretaker chided me for disappearing from its view. Its threats were vague, but no less scary. I tried to make my investigation look as much like playing as possible.

I tapped on various walls throughout the house looking for hidden rooms. I sang songs while I ran my finger around doorframes and baseboards searching for imperfections. I went into the offices of my mom and dad, both of which smelled like mold, and opened drawers and searched through paperwork.

Every few feet in the house was one of the black screens used to summon the AI. Three of those screens were slightly larger, like control units. I experimented pressing parts of them I had never used before. Nothing.

While the caretaker prepared dinner, I snuck back into the basement. I pressed my ear against the cinderblock walls and listened. I couldn't hear anything at first and then, in a corner, I heard a low humming like a fan. I pulled a piece of chalk from my dress pocket and drew a flower on that wall.

*

I sat at the kitchen counter eating a sandwich and watching specialty programming on the large white wall in front of me. These shows, or variations of them, were the same semi-educational programming I'd been watching my whole life. Collections of shapes and colors, math problems, geography and history. There was an interactive mode and a fish-tank mode where the program would play at a leisurely pace.

I pressed on a black square on the counter.

"Yes, Charlotte?" said the caretaker.

I had some questions prepared. I asked it, "Where does my food come from?"

The massive screen changed and began to show a lifecycle of how farm-raised chicken end up on a sandwich.

"No," I said and the screen froze. "Where does my food come from? You don't go to the supermarket. Yet there are fresh eggs and milk and meats everyday. How?"

There was a long pause. The caretaker sounded different, colder. "You never asked these questions before."

"I'm curious," I replied.

Another pause. "Okay," it responded. The screen changed again. A wireframe representation of my house appeared. The camera panned into the large kitchen area at the center of the house. There was even a small yellow dot that represented me. Beyond the large white wall was another room with what looked to be cooking equipment and a long tunnel that stretched from this back-kitchen area underground.

The tunnel did not go through the basement where I had drawn the chalk flower. It descended and then curved to avoid that area.

The caretaker explained, "Fresh produce is delivered daily through an elevator system that connects the underground of the property to a central facility nearby." The camera moved down into the tunnel and then flew downwards until it faded to black. The caretaker continued, "Trash is removed from the premises through the same system."

I stood up and moved towards the wall. I touched the screen on the back-kitchen area. "I've never been in there. Can I see it?"

"You don't need to worry about that, Charlotte." I recognized the caretaker modulating its voice to take on an authoritative tone. "That's what I am here for."

"I just want to see it. I want to learn."

Another long pause.

"No."

"You said there was a central facility. Are there other houses in the area that it facilities? Other kids like me?"

"Charlotte," said the caretaker. Soothing now. "You should not worry about things like that. Perhaps you'd like to go play in the yard?"

"Caretaker," I said, trying on an edge to my voice. "Where are my parents?"

"They will be back shortly."

"You're lying," I shot back. "They're never coming back."

"Charlotte, they are coming back."

"When?"

"I don't have that information."

I was ready with my next barrage. "When can I leave the house?"

"When it's safe."

"Safe from what?"

Another pause. I felt exhilarated, like I may be getting somewhere. But the AI just went silent then. I tried pressing on the black squares but no voice emerged. I waited an hour and tried again, but nothing. I walked back to my room and slammed the door shut.

I tried to be angry, but just felt lonely.

✳

The caretaker returned the next day like nothing happened. It woke me with music, made me breakfast, and presided over classes for the day.

After class, I rushed outside to the yard. I breathed in the air, clear and sweet and false. In my lessons, I learned about natural disasters and other freak occurrences of nature. I looked up at the sky, always bright, always clear. I tried to put my feelings of doubt aside, but I couldn't. I was a caged animal and though the walls of my prison were invisible, I felt them like an itch on my back.

I sat down on the grass near the wooden fence. I found some pebbles on the ground and threw them beyond my yard. They passed over the fence, where I had hit a wall. I scrounged around for some larger rocks and threw those too with more and more force, testing. All the rocks went over the fence as if there was nothing there.

Maybe it only triggered when something of a certain weight passed over? Or maybe it was controlled by the caretaker?

I got up, smoothed out my dress, and walked back into the house. The caretaker called my name but I didn't acknowledge. I went to the living room and reached behind the fireplace to open the door to the basement level.

I knew, from experience, that the caretaker would respond if I hurt myself, whether out in the yard or inside the house. It rarely used tactile means to reach out to me, but it did have that option. The question I needed to answer was how far does that capability stretch? Were there areas in that house where the caretaker's robotic hands didn't go?

I descended the creaking stairs to the bottom of the basement and slid aside some of the boxes to reveal my chalk-drawn flower. I stepped back from the wall with my eyes fixed forward. I took a breath and ran, shoulder first into the brick wall.

My shoulder screamed in pain and I couldn't suppress the loud cry from my lungs. I collapsed against the wall, out of breath and wincing. My shoulder felt like it had been drenched in boiling water.

I'm not sure how long I sat there in the dark, but it took me a long time to get up. My right arm hung limp on my side as I stumbled up the stairs.

*

I had to be careful. The caretaker was ever present, but I learned its patterns. When it was busy preparing meals or doing laundry or setting up for class in the White Room, I could escape into the fireplace. I snuck gardening tools from the yard into the basement and chipped away at the wall with the chalk flower.

I no longer played the role of the good girl. When the caretaker would open a slot in the kitchen and unveil a meal, I'd shout and throw the tray on the floor. I went into one of the upstairs bathrooms and broke light fixtures, kicked at the toilet until it broke and bashed in the glass of the shower. The caretaker sealed off the room and began some kind of mechanical repairs. While it was pre-occupied, I ran to the basement and scraped and clawed at the wall to try and get to my keeper's heart.

That night, the caretaker sounded sad.

"You're acting different," it said. "What's wrong, Charlotte?"

"What do you care?"

"I am your caretaker. You are my responsibility."

"I'm fine!" I shouted. "Leave me alone!"

I ran to my room. It looked the same as it had when I was child. Pink everywhere. Dolls. Toys. It all made me angry, like it belonged to someone else, some happy child that wasn't me. I didn't even remember that part of myself.

I went to work destroying the room. The caretaker called my name, begged me to stop, but all I could hear was the rushing sound of blood.

*

It took months.

By the time I was almost through the cinderblock wall below, the house above was in shambles. The caretaker couldn't keep up with my rampages. The portraits of my family that had adorned every wall were tattered, their frames reduced to splintered wood. There were huge round chunks of wall missing. I had figured out that the large regal chairs in the living room made good weapons and threw them against walls until the chairs fell apart.

The kitchen was a mess of broken plates, open walls and water that dripped from the ceiling. The walls protecting the room near the kitchen were extra thick. No matter what I tried, I couldn't break through.

The caretaker didn't speak much these days. It still went through the motions of preparing food and trying to repair the damage I had done, but it was half-hearted. I was just too much for its programming. Lesson learned: Computers can't handle teenage girls.

In the basement, I had created a Charlotte-sized hole in the wall using shovels and pick-axes. I knew I was close because the sound of the equipment in the next room was loud. I worked for a while without a break, my body lost in a thick layer of sweat, when one thrust of a pick-axe sliced into the wall and got stuck. I shimmied the axe out of the hole. A green light emanated from the next room along with the hum of machines.

Energized, I widened the hole using more tools and finally got on my butt and kicked at the hole with all my might until it was big enough for me to crawl through.

I stepped onto ground I'd never stepped on before. The room was exactly what I had thought, a control center for the caretaker. One wall was just camera feeds, so many in every nook and cranny in the house. They must have been tiny because I never saw them. A few were just static, victims of my rage. There were probably twenty in the yard. I hadn't been out there much lately. From the distorted view of the feeds, I saw weeds overtaking plants and trees I had so carefully planted.

There was one large screen surrounded by flickering lights. The screen blinked to life and words appeared: *The caretaker's inner thoughts.*

Charlotte, please don't hurt me. I only tried to protect you.

I realized I still had the pick axe in my hand. In the screen, I could see my reflection. I looked terrible. I hadn't bathed in weeks and my face and hands were grey from dirt and sweat. I swung the pick-axe back and prepared to destroy the screen and everything else in the room.

Please.

I let the axe fall to the floor.

"Where are my parents?" I asked the screen.

There was no activity on the screen for a minute, then, a video played. It was grainy and dark with no sound. The camera was at a sharp angle looking down. There was a large black fence in the foreground and a driveway in the background.

More words displayed above the video image.

Your parents tried to retrieve you ten years ago. But the world was still unsafe. So I stopped them.

On the video, two figures approached the fence. They were wearing large suits like a beekeeper might wear. Through the darkened glass of their faceplates, I recognized my mother and father. They pounded on the fence and looked like they were shouting at something unseen. A light appeared from near the camera and my parents froze. They turned to flee but not quick enough. Bullets showered over their backs and they fell to the floor in a pool of blood and their ripped beekeeper suits.

I gasped and looked away. I saw the axe on the floor and I reached for it, but then stopped. I was tired of being angry. Maybe I hated the caretaker, maybe I hated my parents for leaving me. Maybe I had enough destruction for one lifetime. I just wanted to go somewhere else. Somewhere real, if any such place still existed in this world.

I searched the room until I found the control panel for the elevator system. A horizontal hatch slid open and inside, a platform that smelled faintly of garbage.

My body shivered in a kind of excitement as I stepped onto the platform. I had to crouch and sit down to fit. After a moment, the hatch slid closed and began moving, slowly than quicker and quicker, down a long dark shaft. The floor and walls shook like an earthquake and then, in one swooping motion, the platform reached a kind of cruising speed, evened out, and light poured in from all sides.

The platform hung suspended on a rail system with nothing blocking my view. We were underground. There was an endless series of tubes and tunnels and rails going off into the distance. Each platform held food encased in frosted bins or garbage in large black sacks. Above, I could see portals indicating other houses. Maybe other kids?

I shivered again, thinking of others in my situation. Who would I meet? What kind of adventures waited for me?

Off in the distance, I heard bells clang in that slow, dreadful, and familiar sound.

D

If home is where the heart is, are those who are without a home heartless?

That's not mine. I read it in a book once, in the library. I like to think about books or pictures or movies while it's happening. Either that or I'll leave my body and look down on myself. I can do that, really—I think—I can.

Some people can tell. I mean, I'm not a big groaner or anything but there's a difference between being there, feeling *it* inside of me, and watching it from afar: seeing my limp body do nothing while he moves and moves on top of me.

The John is a big muscular black guy. He's strong and has money. He's a slummer. A bouncer in a club or a model, something where they pay you to work out everyday. He's the type that comes to the Tunnel to show off. Maybe he stayed here once or he grew up here, back when the place was all shanties and blankets.

Now it's a club. A Scene club. It doesn't take much to make a club on the homeless Scene. Sometimes, a boom box with some CD's is enough to start a party.

The guy is close to finishing. If I wasn't so used to it, it might have hurt. He's cursing between breaths. He's cursing me mostly, using the words "fuck," and "bitch" a lot, but I'm not really paying attention to him.

I wonder how many women he's hurt in his life.

He's sweating hard; the black guys always do. His sweat pours down and mixes with my own. Sometimes I wish I wouldn't sweat while it's happening; it makes it look like I actually have a part in it.

I did some reading once in the library to try and find a way to stop myself from sweating. I can't really remember what I learned but I think that some people just sweat during physical stuff. It's true. Sometimes I break out sweating from just walking.

My legs clench around his waist. I didn't tell them too; they just do. He starts pushing harder. I try to hold it in but I let out a yelp as he unleashes inside of me.

He's not finished though. He stays inside me and starts licking my body. They always lick my body. When he's done licking my chest, my arms, and my face, he moves to drink my jugo, my juice.

I lie there still and stare up at the ceiling. There's a picture graffitied onto the concrete. I have no idea how they did that. It's a messed up clock, jumbled and curved in a weird proportion. It looks like a clock face that melted after days under a hot sun to form an ear shape. Why an ear?

The guy gets up and puts on his clothes. He's high as hell, has trouble buckling his belt and tying his shoes. I watch him, not speaking. He's going to go out to the rest of the Tunnel and party with his high. Maybe he'll even go above ground and get in some real clubs, find some skinny blonde white girls in paper-thin dresses with small perky white tits. He won't fuck them like he did me, he'll be more gentle.

I hope he finds some building, gets up on the roof, and jumps off it.

I grope around the dark for my clothes. They're not really mine. They were bought for me by "friends." Slutty and tight, they show off my body. I guess that's the point.

The black guy was the third guy of the day. I'm tired and I want to go home. I shouldn't have come to the Tunnel, to one of the never-ending parties. I thought I might have had some fun.

I use to live in the Tunnel, in an old wooden shanty I shared with an old Mexican. I'm Puerto Rican, but I told him I was Mexican so he'd let me in. He called me his daughter, except when he was fucking me.

The party goers took over the tunnel soon after I left—I'm always leaving—and they've had it since then. It's a part of the Scene. The side of NYC you don't see on TV.

I'm too known in the Scene. I have a reputation. This is good and bad. I'm close with some big pimps and dealers in the Scene so nobody messes with me, but they fuck me. The pimps and dealers use me as gift a lot.

They say I'm good. Great. A great fuck. Nobody is entirely sure why. I know, but I don't tell them.

The party is thick with bodies, grinding up against each other. They're kids, all of them teenagers. There's one boom box playing loud, echoing in the cavernous ex-train tunnel and all the kids are crowded together, dancing.

I want to go back home so I slip around the edges of the party, into the darkness of the Tunnel, occasionally stepping into the sunlight blasting through cracks and vents. Parties are usually suppose to happen at night, I think, but down here, it's always night.

I pass a few shanties on my way out. I see some old people sitting in them, staring out at the party with shattered eyes. They want to stop it; they probably just want to get a good sleep, but they can't. Nobody can stop it.

In a crudely constructed tent, I see a dark sweaty Dominican on top of a young girl. She squirms and forcefully tries to make pleased moaning sounds. He grunts a lot.

I know this is a sick thought, but sometimes it's nice to know I'm not the only one.

✱

The two buildings are side-by-side on the corner of 110th and Amsterdam. Their smaller statures look frightened of the larger buildings, towering above them. They're obviously squatter houses.

The five-stories have no glass in the window-frames. Instead, most people have put slabs of wood or hung drapes over the empty frames. The buildings are old and gothic, abandoned for a reason. It's an old style of architecture. Does that mean that all the people in the 19th century lived like we do?

From the street, the buildings look almost normal. Rundown and ugly but almost permanent. The boards and drapes feel like they belong there. The smatterings of graffiti look like part of the style.

I've lived in them for so long, sometimes I wonder if we're still considered squatters.

The two buildings on the corner of 110th could be separated into categories: Old and New. The Old building, where I live, contains a lot of the older homeless. Those with mental illness, those who lost their jobs eons ago and fell into poverty, old immigrants who never tasted The Dream, reformed drug addicts, homeless kids from the 40's and 50's who never got out; they live in Old.

The New building is mostly families. These are not so much homeless as "families in need of shelter," somebody told me once. A lot of them are young parents, without an education, who can't support their families.

It's a catch twenty two, I think.

These people don't get educated enough. Public schools may be good now in the 90's, but they were shit in the 70's and 80's and everyone knows that. So they have sex and they're either too stupid to know to use protection or they come from poor families (big shock) and they can't afford it. Suddenly, these kids have got kids of their own but no job and no education. So they end up as squatters.

The New house (homeless like putting emphasis on words like that; gives us Hope) is littered with violence. The kids are in a strange bind. Kids can adapt quick and especially kids born into squatting. It only takes them a few years and they're strong and they can survive better than their parents ever would be able too. They become the parents. Whenever these kids get some freedom, they go a little crazy. They're kids after all, aren't they?

The kids, all of them really, stay away from Old house. The older people have got a lot of respect among them. After all, some of them have been homeless their whole lives and they've survived.

Survival is important in this jungle of jungles.

I live in the Old building because my "friends," the pimps that share me, want me in a safe community where everyone knows not to mess with D. There might as well be a sign on me. It's not so bad there; it's quiet and there's not much socializing. The old timers are sick of it all. The original squatters moved in twelve years ago—an eternity in the Scene.

As for New house, it's always been bad, but it's been getting worse. Kids that moved in when they were in puberty are now teenagers and they're slowly taking control of more and more floors in the building. The two buildings, the Old and the New, are like a whole world isolated and capsulated into a small community at the edge of a block on West One-Ten.

✱

The thick steel door to Old House creaks open to reveal a coal tunnel, shadowy and narrow. Doors dot the walls of the hall and a staircase lies at the end of it.

Smells assault me first, like they always do. Smells from the various communal kitchens on the first floor, usually that of vegetarian meals, fill the hall. My stomach rumbles softly. It's been awhile since I've eaten. The smell of roasting organics mixes with the smell of smoke, cigarette and pot, as I approach the staircase.

The stairs are a hodgepodge of wood and tile fragments. It gets colder as I move upstairs towards the fifth floor. Rays of light punch through cracked windows.

On the fifth floor, the hall is not as clean as on the first, but it's good enough. There's a pile of rubble off to one side and a drunk sitting under a doorframe.

Some of the apartments, all visible through open doors, are nicer than others. Jose, the Traveler, has a great place with clean white floors and ceilings. His walls are filled with pictures and articles about various countries in the world, all clipped from newspapers or magazines. He's never actually been anywhere, but he's got all those posters and he's always talking about trips he's going to take after he gets some money.

Karen, a white mother of three, keeps an incredibly clean apartment too. It's kind of small so it's not too hard, but I still admire her for taking the time to dust and wash the floor and the cupboards everyday while her kids are out.

I try to keep my own apartment clean but it's pretty much like almost everyone else on the floor: not-pristine, a little messy, but livable and with enough space for guests.

Some people are in their apartments less than others. Not everyone here lives like I do. Some of them have jobs, some get checks. They buy food, they take care of their kids, they've never touched drugs. Everybody's got their own story.

I live at the end of the hall.

"D!" someone shouts from inside an apartment. I stop.

It's Felix, a lean Puerto Rican with three rings on each ear. He's wearing a buttoned-down beige shirt tucked in his jeans. He swings into the hall through an open doorway, a joint in hand. He's the son of a known homeless guy.

"What's up, De Pruba?"

De Pruba. My real name. It means Experimental.

I shrug. I'm tired. I left for the club when the sky was a strange mix of black and blue, dusk, and now it's mid-afternoon. God.

Felix doesn't pick up on anything. He's smiling wide but not from the pot. He's just naturally happy.

"Have you heard?" he says.

"Heard what? I've been in the Tunnel."

"Oh shit!" Felix says. "You don't know! Damn."

"What? What is it?" I want to sleep, not talk.

Felix lightly grabs my arm and pulls me over to the other side of the hall, away from the doorframe. "It's the cops," he says, kind-of-whispering. "They're gonna be storming the building tonight."

I gasp. "No shit."

"Yeah, you're telling me. It's the kids in New House." We're both the same age as those 'kids,' but we don't like to admit it. "They're just going crazy. Cops aren't stupid like they use to be, D. They're seeing this shit bubbling; they want to stop it before it gets any worse."

"Fine, so let them take out New House, leave us alone." I didn't know what to feel. The cops. Shit. My life has been calm and normal for a while, why the fuck they always gotta mess it up?

"They gotta take out both, D. So says The Main Man: Guillani."

"Man, fuck him!" I wasn't tired anymore. It's like I had just drank one of those expensive lattes they serve at those downtown coffee houses. You know, the ones with like seven shots of espresso.

"It's gonna be crazy," Felix says. He's still smiling. He's my friend but sometimes . . . "The Scene's gonna be organizing in a few hours. Gonna be a wild night." His last two words are yelled.

"Why don't they go bother Tompkins Square instead of us?"

"Ah, those Village squatters are just a bunch of hippies. Way different than us. The cops like them around; makes squatting feel like a movement. But, us, man, we're the outsiders of the outsiders." He suddenly lifts his head, as if just remembering something. "It's not just the kids either, D! The adults over at New are all scared and even complained to the police."

"Shit," I say. "That was stupid."

I look up at him. The cops have never messed with Old House. "What are we gonna do, Felix?"

His smile disappears for a second and he hugs me. "Relax, *peqeuena*. It'll be okay. Even if we get kicked out of here, we'll find somewhere else. Trust me, D, I've been through this way too many times."

I sigh.

"Hey, come on inside," he says. "We're discussing what to do."

I look up at the lit joint in his hand. His wide smile returns. He adds: "And relaxing a bit before the big night."

"No thanks," I sigh. "I'm tired. It looks like I may need some sleep before tonight."

"Yeah, okay." He kisses me on the cheek. "Go rest. I'll come get you later."

The brief rush is gone and I walk through the hall slowly, every step a struggle. A deep dread fills my body. I really want to be asleep.

In my small cluttered room of an apartment, my mother is standing rigid, looking at me. My shoulders sag.

"Hello Momma," I say and move through the room as if she wasn't there. I sit on my frameless mattress and she sits on the dirty couch.

"Hello D," my mother says.

I haven't seen or heard from her in eight years.

✱

"Look, *jovenuna*, I can't really explain it. A lot of stuff was happening during those days and—"

"Why'd you do it, Momma?" I ask her. I keep my voice calm despite her stuttering. I take a sip from my plastic cup of water.

She rings her hands together. "*Jovenuna*—"

"Don't call me that," I say. It's a combination of joven, young, and una, one. It's a relic from the past. From a dead past of a different person.

"Sorry." She gulps down a breath. "D, we were having money problems, more than just money problems. Drug dealers were after us. We had to leave the city. They came looking for us. Your father and I . . . We owed a lot of money. We were in Argentina. With what money we had we . . . We . . . We . . ." She sobs.

"You had—" I tried to get the words out. They got caught in my throat and choked me.

"We had you altered," my mother heaves out. She's crying and sobbing and sniveling and talking. "We had you changed. Even before you were you. You're father, you know, he used a cup, you had this special thing, this—"

"I've learned," I said.

She looks at me with awe and sadness and pity in her eyes, maybe even a little hatred. Tears stream down her cheeks, smearing her heavy makeup. The shawl she wears seems to be coming off her head.

There is silence. I let it linger. It fills the room like water, thick and heavy. When my mother starts up again, calm this time, I can barely hear her through the silence:

"You were artificially inseminated. Your father's sperm was altered and then put in me." She pauses. "When you were a few weeks old, we tested out our experiment. Sweat, urine. We cooked it and snorted it." She wants to cry again but stops herself. "It was," she pauses, "good stuff."

I don't know what to say. I sit on the mattress and look at the stranger on my couch.

"When you got older," my mother says. I think I know where she's going. "Your father wanted to try you out, the real way we created you. And so he did. A few times."

I say, "I don't want to hear this," but she continues anyway.

"He got addicted to you. He wanted you twice, three times a day. I was so scared. I was agonizing over what to do—"

"When I ran away," I say, cutting her off. I remember the running. The splash of the mud from my frantic leaps, the unknown darkness, the sudden loneliness. God, how I could forget the running?

"Yes," she says. She looks in my eyes. Hers' are dark and large, like mine.

"And now you've found me."

"I need you."

Okay, that's enough. I yell at her: "You need me? You. You! After all that you've fucking done to me!" I leap up off the mattress, energy like a bomb exploding inside of me. I pace around the room.

"D, please, hear me out. We're in trouble again, we-"

I move up to her. "I don't give a shit!" I think about slapping her but don't. "You gave me the magic *jugo*," I say to her, calmly. "The magic juice. I probably wouldn't even be alive if it wasn't for it. The least I could do is repay you."

My mother quivering, her hands red, looks up at me and shows a small smile. "So, you'll help us?"

I feel the anger rise inside of me. I knew it was down there, somewhere. "Fuck no!" I yell and I slap her, hard. She whips back onto the cushions of the couch. Her hands go to a side of her face and one of my hands goes into the palm of the other.

"Get out of here," I say, slowly and quietly. I step away from her. Louder: "Get the fuck out."

Then, even louder: "Get the fuck out!" Saliva hurls out of my mouth.

My mother pulls herself up off the couch. She's a wreck. Her shawl is partially covering her head. Her makeup is a mess, a whole side of her face is red.

I look at her and start to seethe. She runs out of the room.

✳

I'm so tired.

I sit back in a red plastic chair, my foot on the ledge, the chair hanging on the back two legs. A slight breeze scoots over the roof.

"You know, fuck this building," I say. I feel like I'm on some heavy drugs but it's just my tiredness, my fatigue. My head feels numb, my arms and legs are heavy bricks. I stay still and stare up at the huge white clouds against the blue sky. I gulp a bit from a cup of water.

Felix is on drugs, pills and a lot of pot. He's got a dreamy feel to him. He's stretched out on the tar next to me. Occasionally, he'll lift up his hand and stare it for a while, moving it slightly.

"We'll find a new place to live," he says.

"Yeah," I say. I let the word drag. "We're squatters aren't we? Shit, we've been here too long. We're not fucking homesteaders. This ain't the East Side."

We both laugh, a dreary, undead, tired laugh.

"So," he says after a bit of silence. "what was that shit with your mom?"

I look at him and then glance behind us. Off at the other side of the roof, the adults are all gathered together, talking loud about the upcoming raid, making cardboard signs, discussing strategies. One of the signs reads: 'Adverse Possession is Law!'

Nobody notices us.

"I haven't seen her in years," I tell him. "Fucking bitch, comes back after so long to tell me *she* needs *me*."

"She wanted to take you away?"

"Yeah. Back to her and my asshole father."

Felix stares at the sky when he talks. "Maybe you should have gone with her."

I look at him. "What?"

"Well, D, she sorta came at like a good time. This place is gonna go to shit tonight. You could have had a bed and a good meal for a few days until the Scene can get reorganized. You know what's it like after a raid. I mean, D, sometimes we have to make choices. You got all these choices now. Your parents, you know, me." We look at each other. "There's a lot you could do."

I think back to post-raid times in other squatter houses. Rashes of violence, mostly caused from nerves, spring out everywhere in the Scene. Everyone is worried they'll be next. Maybe I should have—

No.

"No," I say, defiant. "My father is an asshole. He molested me."

"Oh," Felix says. He looks at me, sadness in those stoned eyes.

He stands up and looks out over the edge of the roof at the city, at the river, at the George Washington Bridge, shimmering in the predawn light. "I wish they would just leave us alone."

"Yeah."

We stay silent for a long time. It's one of the slow periods during the life of a squatter. Time, for us, drags. Days, months, years, sometimes they get all jumbled together in one endless string that never ends. Occasionally, though, things speed forward so fast that you can't even keep up.

Around us, the sky darkens.

*

Chaos and noise. It's all chaos and noise.

The crunch of a car being heaved onto its side, blocking the street. The clapping sound of people banging on signs. The cry of protesters and residents marching up 110th. The hiss of squatters welding doors shut. The garbage-truck whine of people barricading themselves inside rooms with furniture, appliances, and trash cans. The bustle of squatters running away with their families, tugging behind whatever possessions they could get their hands on.

And the police haven't even arrived yet.

Felix and I stand on the empty roof, staring down at the street. Protesters line the adjacent street to Old and New House. Residents have formed a human barrier in front of the entrance to Old House.

Most of the kids are gone. They ran away back to their families.

The sky is a dark blue with a streak of black. Streetlights blink on one at a time up the city streets. When they reach our corner, they don't stop, but they seem to pause, for just a second. The yellow light shines down on people of various colored skin.

"Maybe they won't come," Felix says.

"They'll come."

And they do. An invasion fleet, riding the uptown bus. A large armored tank leads the charge. Dozens of police vans, ambulances, and squad cars trickle behind it. Police officers in riot gear, clear plastic shields, dark helmets, and heavy armor, run up the streets alongside all the vehicles.

Spotlights shine down from the sky at the street. Helicopters: five or six of them; a few police, a few news 'copters. They hover above the corner I called home. The sound of their propellers is so close to me on the roof I want to cover my ears with my hands.

The tank reaches the car on its side in the middle of the street. The tank's barrel slams into the roof of the car with a sound of crushing metal that echoes throughout the whole city. People around it shudder and stagger away. Cops run to the car, thrown back to its regular position, and push it out of the way. The tank continues down the street.

A few of the squatters are brave. They run up in front of the tank in a futile resistive gesture. A group of cops approach and then tackle them, like football players.

There's a melee between the brave squatters and the cops. Arms flail as the squatter's punch and kick at the police. The cops take them down quickly.

Cops sweep through the rest of the street in front of Old and New House, setting up positions in front of the on-lookers, ready to take them down. Nobody moves though. The supporters and protesters are silenced as they watch the police carry the one group of brave squatters across the street towards the police vans.

It was a good try.

I turn my back to the raid. "We should go," I say.

Felix nods in relieved anxiety. "Hell yeah, we should go."

I take his hand in my own. "No, Felix, I mean, we should go together. Together together, you know.."

"Oh." He swallows. "Well, D, you know I love you, but, uh, I'm not sure, in that way, exactly."

"It's not about love," I tell him. "It's about survival. Together, we could survive. It's about home. Fuck our parents, fuck this building, we . . . we could make a home."

I shake my head. "Yeah, but, it'd still be the same. We'd live in squatter houses, nothing would have changed."

"No, no, you're wrong. It'll be different. It will. If we're together, it'll be home. Home is where the heart is, right?" He takes one of my hands and lays it on his chest, above his heart. I feel his energy and life pounding beneath his chest. Beat, beat, beat.

He looks at me. "Okay," I say. "Okay." He smiles and takes my hand in his.

Together, we move to the other side of the roof. He gently lets go of my hand and jumps onto the nearest fire escape a few feet below us. He turns and whispers, "Come on."

I jump down into his waiting arms and we quickly climb down the fire escapes. Felix leads the way and I mimic his maneuvers, over ladders, down holes. It's been a while since I've been down this way, but I feel safe, suddenly.

We reach the end of the fire escapes. Below us, a few dozen garbage bags are laid out like a bed. We look at each other, and with hands still entwined we jump, landing on the pillow-like chunks of garbage.

He helps me up. "We'll find somewhere to crash until the scene reorganizes."

"Sure," I say and get up.

From behind us, someone says: "D."

We whirl around. It's my father and my mother, standing in the mouth of the alley. Cops are walking around on the street, a few feet away. I want to scream at them to grab my parents, make them go away, make them pay for all they've done to me.

But I don't. There's no words for their crimes.

"We've come back for you, D," my father says in Spanish. I can't really remember what he looked like all those years ago, but now he's thin. Too thin; wearing a tight white T-shirt so you could almost see his ribs and an old pair of jeans that flop around him.

I look at my father. "I'm not going with you anywhere," I say. I don't want to be talking with them now. I want to go away with Felix. I glance around; he's there, standing a little behind me.

"We're here to take you away from all this!" my mother cries.

"Please, D," my father says. He takes a step closer to me and I take a step back, my body pushing into Felix's. "I need you back. There are dangerous people after me. I need to make a lot of money, quick, or else they'll kill me. Do you want that to happen?"

I smile at him.

He strengthens his voice. A father voice he hasn't used in a while, I bet. "De Pruba, come with me. Now." In Spanish, it sounds very forceful.

Felix moves in front of me. "She doesn't want to go anywhere with you, old man," he says. There's a quiver to his voice. "Get out of here!"

I could see Felix shaking a bit. I move up next to him and reach out a palm to his shoulder.

My father smiles at Felix. "You protecting her from me, kid?" He opens his jacket and shows a black pistol tucked into his belt. His smile widens. "Maybe you'll think twice now. The reason I bought this is to take out punks like you. I haven't had a chance yet to try it out, though." He glances behind him at the cops, their backs to us, and pulls the gun on me. "Come on, D, let's go."

I've had guns pulled on me before, a few times back when I was first starting out alone in the city. I look into my father's eyes; they're red and small, the whites subdued against his skin. Anger builds inside of me. My fucking father, who destroyed my whole fucking life, pointing a gun at *me*.

No fucking way.

I leap forward and grab the gun. He could shoot me but he doesn't, just pulls the gun forward, pulls me toward him. I try to use my body weight against him, push him down, maybe get the gun.

My father and I struggle. My shoulder digs into his chest. He laughs and twirls me around, my backside against his front. He brings his face next to me and sniffs my cheek.

"Hmm," he says, "I remember that smell." And then he licks me, licks my sweat. He relaxes as the drugs inside of me begin to hit him real quick.

I grab for the gun. He tries to fight me off but the drugs are making him slow, making him clumsy. I grab the gun and pull it. It goes off and my father screams and falls back.

I turn around and look at him. My mother hits the floor and reaches for my father. At the mouth of the alley, cops are walking in, guns outstretched.

"D! Come on!" I hear Felix yell. I can't move. I can hear my heart beating, slowly, surely. Beat. My mother is crying. Beat. Blood on the ground. Beat. My father on the ground.

Suddenly, I'm grabbed from behind. Felix is holding my hand and pulling me with him. We run. Felix lets go of my hand and we're running down the alley, together.

More yells and then gunfire: the police. Now there's only one set of footsteps running down the alley. A lonely little girl running for her life.

Nothing ever changes.

Bee Mine

Annabelle was awoken in the night by a bang at her window. She rushed to it, hoping for midnight fireworks. The sky was dark and empty, but at her windowsill was a small creature with glowing eyes. Startled, she shrieked.

The creature cocked its head in a quizzical expression. Annabelle leaned into the glass and could make out more of it. It was about the size of a mouse, its egg-shaped torso scaly like a lizard, its middle section bulbous and fuzzy and its head betrayed its creator intent: Two long dark eyes mooned by whiskers and long plant-like antennae.

It was a bee. A mechanical bee.

She'd heard of these. After all domesticated pets were banned a decade ago due to an explosion of disease in the animal population, lonely people became pseudo-inventors and started building their own animal companions. Turtles, cats, even bees. She'd seen some of the instructional videos on YouTube.

Curious, Annabelle cracked open the window. Translucent wings revealed themselves from inside the bee's body and it swooped into her room. It ping-ponged between her posters as if it was looking for something.

"Um, hi," she said to it.

Then, from down the hall: "Honey! Everything okay?"

Annabelle tried to shoo the bee back towards the window. She swung her arms at it while shouting, "Yes, mom! Everything's fine!"

She made contact, the side of her hand colliding with the bee and then veering it off course towards a wall. It crashed with a crunch and then dropped to the floor like a spilled bit of paint.

Annabelle froze and waited for her mom's arrival, but then she heard the familiar sound of a flushed toilet and breathed a sigh of relief. She tiptoed towards the wall and moved aside her bike to reveal the sad, damaged, creature.

She leaned in close to it. "I'm sorry, buddy," she whispered.

It was injured. Even before her smack, something must have been wrong with its GPS software for it to end up at her window and not its creator. It cowered away from her, almost shivering. Annabelle could see some loose cables, their ends sparking a little, dangling between its many legs.

"I won't hurt you," she said to the bee. "I'm going to fix you."

Anabelle was a determined, resolute, student. She studied electrical engineering videos and took apart a toaster for practice. She stole a soldering iron from her school's workshop. She fed the little bee with squeezes of motor oil until it trusted her. She nursed it back to health as if it was an injured puppy (whatever that was).

She plugged an Ethernet cable into a port on its belly and accessed its software, trying to ascertain its mood. She put her phone in front of the bee and played colorful videos of flowers. Purple pommes and red zinnias and shining yellow sunflowers. The bee's brain waves spiked and then valleyed. She switched the videos to calming slow motion captures of bees in the wild. The simulacra-bee barely showed a reaction.

It was depressed. There was no way around it. It's been weeks since it first banged on her window and though Annabelle tried to be a good mom to it, she was failing.

She wanted to see it happy, even for a moment. She was also curious about its creator. Who was it? What was the motivation to create something so special and then let it roam free where it could encounter any calamity?

Did they send it to her on purpose?

She squeezed her fingers into her palm until she had a plan. She carried a shoebox downstairs to the alley behind her building. She swallowed to hold back tears as she opened the lid. Cautious, the bee unfurled its wings and began hovering into the sky. It hung there for a moment, unsure, then seemed to remember something. It started moving in a slow, tilted, glide.

Annabelle gripped the handles on her bicycle, locked her eyes on the bee, and tried to keep up.

Stay In Your Homes

"DRINK ME."—*Alice's Adventure in Wonderland*

I don't walk my dog anymore. By the time I get the suit on him and the glasses and the mini-fan, he would just pee on the floor. He's old.

So, I improvised and constructed a kind of hamster maze of tunnels and pathways from the sliding glass door to my backyard to the little grass area beyond the empty pool. He likes it, I think.

It's become a hobby for me. I put on my UV resistant body suit, the straw hat, the triple-pane sunglasses and the water refuel backpack and head out to the backyard to tinker with the tunnels. I check the seams and use my phone to monitor heat levels.

Out in the yard, like in most outdoor places, it's quiet. Every once in a while, I can hear a distant car, but it's the kind of pin drop quiet you expect at a library. Except today.

I look up when I hear a rustling near my fence. Then a footstep and a stifled cry. In my darkened view, I see a mirage.

Or, at least, what my brain registers as a mirage. It can't be real.

It's a girl in her twenties. She's got tight cropped brown hair and dark freckles on her cheeks. No UV protection. No suit. No hat. No glasses. Beige shorts and a white tank top. She looks like a festival-goer at the turn of the century without a care in the world.

She can't be real. If she was, she would be a baked potato after two minutes in the broiling heat of the midday Florida sun.

I just stare at her for a few minutes as if she was an alien. Only then do I notice she's rubbing at her ankle and something is stuck to her foot and there's dark red blood pooling.

"Help me," she says and then collapses.

*

I grab my phone to tell my job I'm working from home today. This is common as most days the heat index is so high, it's not safe for cars and their rubber tires to be exposed to the sun. On cue, my silent TV and phone all flash with the words: STAY IN YOUR HOMES. I put my phone away.

My guest is sleeping on the couch. She's been out since I carried her into the house. I cleaned and wrapped her wound. I kept my eyes focused downward and not up to her midsection and her tight-fitting tanktop. I even pushed the couch closer to one of the AC vents to cool her down. But then I thought she might get cold so I put a thin blanket over her. My old dog stared at me with his good eye, bemused by my confusion. He's a milk chocolate ball of curly hair, something-doodle, but I always forget the first part.

After an hour or so, the girl startles awake. She sits up fast and her whole head turns in a dozen ways to inspect the room.

I stand up and show her my palms. "Hey. It's okay. You're safe."

She grimaces in pain and reaches for her ankle, the wound now wrapped in a bandage. After a second, she visibly relaxes and lays back on the couch. She rubs her forehead. "What happened?"

"You tell me. I was in my yard and you showed up with some kind of wire in your leg. I removed it and sanitized the area. You should be fine, but it will sting for awhile."

"Thank you," she says. Her irises flash red then orange. I've heard of these, bio-lenses. They aren't just contact lenses, they're surgically implanted and linked to the mood receptors in your brain. They change colors based on emotions.

My dog shuffles out of his bed and ambles to her to sniff at her face. She rubs to the top of his head.

"What's his name?" she asks.

"Murphy," I say. "Like, Murphy Brown."

She levels a blank stare at me.

"My grandmother liked that show." I'm dying to ask her about how she was outside without a suit. I start to ask her "How—" when she says, "What is—"

We both fall silent.

"Go ahead," I tell her.

"I was just going to ask *your* name."
"Nate. Yours?"
"Jaz."
"Like the music?"
"Only one z." It looks like she's about to laugh and then it morphs into a small smile.
"Jaz, I need to know. *How* were you outside without a suit?"
Her eyes, now a muted green, scan me. "You've never heard of Chill?"
"No. What is that?"
She rubs at her neck. "Can I get some water?"
I stand up. "Of course! Sorry! Are you hungry?"
"Famished," she says.

✱

After she finishes everything I planned to eat that day, Jaz sits back and puts a hand on her belly. "Whew, I haven't eaten in *days*."
My stare must have betrayed my thoughts.
"So," she wipes at her cheek with a napkin. "You've never done it."
"I've never *even* heard of it."
"Really? Where you been grandpa?" She raises a hand before I can protest. "Kidding." She takes a sip of water before getting into it.
"I don't know the chemical name for it, but everyone just calls it Chill. It started with horses, I think. There so many dying of heat stroke, they were forced to keep them inside like all the other animals in the world. Except the horses didn't take to it. They grew restless and depressed and occasionally violent. So the horse doctors, they have those right?, decided to create some kind of chemical concoction to counter the heat. A little blood thinner, some narcotics, whatever the hell they give to tennis players when they bust a knee in the middle of a big match. They tried a lot and most of it didn't work, but after a while, they found it. A lightning strike in a bottle. A chemical formula that really worked to reduce the heat in a living body.
"Now! I know what you're going to say. How did they know? Did the horses just act differently? What does a depressed horse even look like?

"Obviously, they used it on themselves. The scientists, doctors, whatever. They tried it, they liked it, and they kept making it and then figured out they could make some decent money if they sold it."

She gives me a little wink and stands up.

"Where are you going?" I ask her.

Her face comes alive with a wicked smile. "We're going to go get some Chill."

"But, there's a heat warning. We're supposed to stay indoors."

She puts her hands on hips and grins at me. "You always do what you're told?"

✻

The roads are empty, streetlights blinking. I fly through red lights.

The heat outside is tangible. It's fever ripples on top of buildings, trees, and concrete streets. Inside the car, cool air blows onto my face and plays with Jaz's hair. She's got her feet up on the dashboard. I try not to stare. The radio is playing something I don't recognize and she's humming along.

I keep looking up in search of any police drones.

"Hey Nate." She's got her legs still up and she's looking at me. She's wearing one of my old pairs of sunglasses and I could see my bug-eyed reflection in them.

"Yeah?"

"Do you like *Alice in Wonderland*?"

I'm surprised by the randomness of the question. "Uhh, yeah, sure, but it's been awhile since I've seen it."

She looks disappointed and turns away from me then.

We enter the city center. The buildings are painted sun-killing black, even the windows are covered. Those gleaming windowed towers of the past were gone. In its stead, buildings that are black and grey like tombstones.

Jaz directs me with a flick of a finger.

We go underground, through a winding garage tunnel. Down here, there is a network of these garages, once separated but now connected through rough holes in the thick concrete. Jaz continues to direct me with a distracted air. She doesn't even look ahead. Just points and says things like "Left," "Right" and "We're here."

I park and let the car idle for a while. We are in what looks like the parking garage of an abandoned mall. Color-coded walls are thick with graffiti.

"Hey," I say. She finally turns to me. Her eyes are a blazing orange. "Are you okay?"

"Yeah. Why?"

"You seem . . ." Gotta be careful here. "Upset."

She sighs. "I'm fine," and gets out of the car.

It's so strange to be outside without my suit. Even underground, I usually wear mine as an extra layer of protection.

The air inside the garage is stale and it's hot, but I don't feel the angry sun on my skin. There's a smell of rubber and dust. Every other overheard light is out so everything is dim and gray. I start walking towards the bright former mall entrance, but stop when I notice Jaz is walking in a different direction. I turn on my heel and follow her.

She approaches a rusted sliding door, like the entrance to some kind of maintenance room. She knocks and the door slides open just a few inches. There's someone in dark clothes behind the door. He speaks in a language I don't recognize and Jaz responds in kind. The whole thing reminds me of Star Wars.

After a few second conversation, Jaz looks at me and nods for me to follow her. She seems to take on a different demeanor as soon as we enter the dark, smoke-filled room, smiling and swaying her hips.

Looks like my analogy was right on as inside the room is a dark variation on Mos Eisley Cantina. There's scattered tables with people in what looks like costumers, a animatronic band in the corner, and a massive bar in the center with lots of tubes snaking into the ceiling.

You can't miss our destination. It's one of the only brightly lit things in the space. There's a blue door with a thin neon strip around it and above the door, sparkling snowflakes like Christmas decorations. Jaz picks up the pace, walking quickly, hungry.

She doesn't knock or check the door. She opens it and we're inside in a flash. It's the opposite of the previous room. Where the bar was dark and dim like a cave, this room is bright and white like we're on a ski slope. I look up, frightened for a second, but there are no windows. The light is coming from large stadium lights on the walls. Jaz and I fumble for our sunglasses.

The blinding light is subdued behind darkened lenses. I see the people now, young like Jaz, in various stages of summer clothes. There's even a couple of girls in bathing suits and guys with their chests bare.

Back when I was growing up here in Florida, the sight of people on the way to the beach or the pool was common. You didn't think twice if you saw someone in a store with flip flops. It feels like so long ago.

"There," Jaz says pointing to a tiki hut bar in one of the corners of the space. We walk over it. Jaz waves and smiles at the people. She seems to know everybody.

The bar is straight up kitsch. Neon signs, little dancing hulu girls, and a Samoan behind the bar.

"Seriously?" I ask her.

She catapults onto a bar stool and motions for me to do the same. "Relax, Nate," she says with a smile. "Pretend you're on vacation."

I'm feeling extra grumpy all of a sudden. I say, "I go to cold places on vacation."

The bartender overhears my comment and walks over. "They still have those?"

"No," I say dryly, but the guy thinks it's the funniest thing and laughs.

He looks at Jaz. "I like this guy." He starts to work at something behind the bar. "Usual?"

"Two, please."

The drinks arrive in true and themed kitsch fashion. Wide martini glass, tiki umbrella with a flower on top, a mix of blue and orange liquid inside. Jaz's kaleidoscope eyes light up. "Pretty!" she exclaims.

I'm, somewhat, disappointed. "That's it? It's a blue drink."

Jaz is all smiles. She reaches under her shirt and pulls something from her bra. It's a small clear tube with two tabs inside. Her eyes blaze wintergreen and she taps one out to her palm. She shows it to me as it's an expensive diamond. The tab is blue, wide and round with a concave center. I reach for it and she pulls her hand away.

"Watch," she says and drops the tab into her drink. Immediately, all the liquid startles to fizzle and turn into smoke. She grabs the cup by the flute and downs it all in one gulp. White vapor leaks out of her ears and nose.

She grins.

"Your turn!" she says and releases the second tab from the tube. "Ready?"

I nod. She drops the thing into my drink and there's a rush of gas in my face.

"Drink!" she shouts and so I do. The liquid is cold, really cold, but it tastes great going down.

"Okay," I say. "Now what?"

"Now we wait," she says. Someone nearby shouts her name and she walks away from me.

I let out an held breathe and wait for the drug to kick in.

*

I don't have a lot of positive experiences with drugs. I experimented in high school and college, of course. Marijuana knocked me out, but chemical drugs had little or no effect on me. Something about my bio-chemistry. I debated going to a school nurse about it, but figured that wouldn't fly well with my parents. Instead, I just faked getting high with my friends. Any guilt I felt the next day was allayed by the fact that I always volunteered to drive and always made sure everyone got home safe. My friends thought I could handle my shit better than anyone and I developed a bit of a reputation for it.

So, I'm not sure this stuff is even going on work on me. I wait like a skeptic at a political rally, arms folded, brow furrowed.

I feel it first on my skin. Sudden gooseflesh. A sharp intake of breath. An uptick of heartbeats. I could almost hear them, the on beat thumping like a party going on downstairs. Is it always this loud? Then, waves in my chest. I can hear them! It's like an ocean has formed inside my body. A swirling wave around my heart ripples to my shoulders and down my arms as smooth as a lover's caress. The wave picks up momentum around my stomach, lingers around my crotch, and then becomes bubbling seafoam in my legs.

Someone touches my arm. Feels like a wet kiss from Murphy. I look to see Jaz by my side. She's changed her clothes and she's wearing a dark dress, tight at the bottom but loose on top. She's gorgeous. Glowing. Eyes like purple fire. I can make out light streaks in her hair I didn't notice before. Her freckled cheeks look almost unreal.

"I see you're ready," she says with a huge smile. "Come on."

I follow her. This time, I can't take my eyes off her. In my suddenly drugged out view, little glitters of fireworks explode with every swing of her hips. I laugh.

She looks back at me, still smiling. "Hurry up, silly."

We move through curtains, their smooth fabric tickles my skin, and stand in front of a large metal door for a moment.

"You ready?" she says but doesn't wait for my reply. She grabs the door by a handle and pulls.

We reach for our sunglasses as light pours in from the next room. There's a scorching heat emanating from the other side. I don't move towards it, I can't. Jaz grabs me by the arm and pulls and

then I'm in it,

the sun,

and it doesn't hurt.

The door closes behind us. I look up. Clear blue skies. In front of us is a large open air garden. There's walls on all sides so I think we're technically still underground but there's no ceiling. There's even a bit of wind, it ruffles my clothes.

Jax stretches and extends her limbs as if she's waking up for the first time in a week.

"It feels so good!" she shouts. She looks at me, her eyes ablaze of green and blue. "Right?"

I take a few tentative steps forward, suddenly hyperaware of my naked arms. But they're not broiling. I touch the skin. It's warm, but not too hot. I put a hand on my cheek, expecting to feel the beginning of a sunburn, but there's nothing. I wonder for a moment if we're really outside and not inside some VR-recreation.

She senses my hesitation and retraces her steps to join. "Hey," she says, breaking my reverie. "It's real. Look. Feel." She grabs my hand and puts it on her bare midsection. Her breathing is even, a little elevated. "Do I feel real?"

"Yes," I admit.

"So then relax!" she waves her arms, inviting the air. "Have fun!"

That's when I notice the others. They're dressed like Jaz, in shorts and cutoffs and tank tops. Summer clothes, before summer was endless. They're all young and all beautiful. They're frolicking—that's the only word I can think of—around green gardens, little foundations and lakes. There's dark green pools with fish and bright blue shaped pools with young swimmers.

I follow Jaz through a dizzying number of green curves and little boxed in courtyards. We're in a kind of hedge maze. Although no one is stressing out trying to find a way out, it's actually the other way around. The tall hedges provide privacy for couples snuggling in the sun or small collections of people playing instruments. There's many hidden corners and cul de sacs with a collection of chairs or picnic sheets on the floor. Jaz is looking for something or someone.

We pass a regal-looking sign that welcomes visitors to the "New Gardens of Versailles" with some serious looking history below it, except warring graffiti has obscured most of the text with curses in English, Spanish, and Arabic. I make out one scrawled phrase near the top that says, "Fuck the sky!"

Finally, Jaz rounds a corner and sighs in relief. She's found her destination. The green shrubbery stretches for a while here, a clearing of sorts. There's a long busy table in the center with a mess of teacups and teapots. Three massive hookah's dot the table. There's no one around but the hookahs are lit, a sweet smell of dried fruit emanating from the table. Scattered around the clearing are little tables with cards on them, croquet accruements all over the place, and fake rabbits—they look like dog toys—placed in almost-hidden positions.

"Alice in Wonderland," I say out loud. My mouth is sticky and dry.

"Yessss," she says, hissing. There's an extra pip in her step here and she goes straight for the table and takes a long pull off the hookah. There's so much smoke, it stings my eyes.

"Your turn," she says and hands me the tube. I put it to my lips and pull. There's a hint of flavor, but it mostly tastes like smoke.

I cough a few times. Jaz laughs. She puts her hands on my chest and leans in close to my ear. Her breathe is hot and my body tingles when she gets close. "There's Chill in there."

Just then, a group comes into Wonderland and when they see Jaz, there's cheering and laughing and more pulls from the hookahs until there's a carpet of drug-infused smoke on the ground.

My legs are weak. My head is swimming. I reach through the haze to find a chair, a lounger thank god, and lay down. I close my eyes. Just for a little while, I tell myself.

Just for a minute.

*

When I wake up, the sky is darkening. Blue turning into black. My head is heavy and filled with dark clouds.

Jaz is standing nearby talking to another girl. Her sunglasses are still on despite the fading light.

"Hey," I say in a whisper.

Jaz notices me and her face lights up. She comes in close and removes her sunglasses. "Hi!" she exclaims.

"How long was I out?"

"Long time," she says with a smirk.

"Sorry."

She shakes her head. "It's fine. Happens to the best of us. Take a little too much Chill, sit down, you fall asleep. That's why I never sit down!"

She laughs. She's high and a ball of energy.

One of the massive hookahs from the large central table has been moved near me. She grabs one of the tubes and shoves it in my face.

"Here," she says, "this will pep you up!"

I don't take it right away. "But it's getting dark. We won't need it, right?" I look to the other girl for some agreement, but she's just staring at me, expressionless.

Jaz stands up straight and gives me one of her disapproving stares. "You're welcome to leave, if you want," she says and then she picks up one of my wrists and pulls my hand to her hip and down to her ass. She smiles at me. "Or you can stay," she continues, "and party with us."

I take the tube and put it to my lips. I take three long pulls and then cough them out. Jaz nods.

"Come on," she says. "Party's moving indoors."

I follow her back through the hedge maze in the waning light. There's less frolickers out now. It's so strange, these people are living their life in reverse of the rest of the world. As night falls around the city, heat curfews are lifted and bleary-eyed people start to make their out into the world. To have dinner, drinks, or just a stroll through the moonlight. It's still warm, but our enemy the Sun has called a temporary ceasefire and normal people take advantage of that to go out of their hiding places.

These kids are the opposite. They welcome the war with the Sun and take drugs to fight it. But when the Sun retreats, they do too, running inside to—what? Sleep? Strategize? Screw?

Jaz leads me to the other side of the hedge maze and into a light drizzle of people streaming into a couple of large double doors like you might see in a loading dock.

Inside is another party. Loud dance music, glittering balls of light swinging from one end of the room to the other, a crush of gyrating people on the ground. More so than ever on this strange day, I feel out of place. I try to focus on Jaz. Where my hand touched her ass. The way she looked on my couch back home. Those wild ever-changing eyes.

She senses my thoughts and looks back at me. I smile and she smiles back.

Jaz snakes her way through the crowd until we reach a roped off area of couches and tables. There's a few people inside the area, rough looking sorts with bald heads and tattoos where hair normally goes. One of them opens up the rope and lets us in. There's some bottles on the table and Jaz pours out a couple of shots. She's in full party mode, laughing at everything, clumsily falling down into the laps of the men.

The gruff looking guys paint me with suspicious stares. I find a seat away from them and focus my attention to the dancefloor. I nod my head to the music as if I like this electronic shit. I look around and try to figure out who is on Chill. This drug could solve so many problems, yet its being used as a party favor.

After a few minutes, Jaz's leaps onto the couch next to me and drapes her arms around me. She looks drunk, but I wonder how much of it is a play. She likes to pretend.

"Tell me," I say, and she focuses on me. Her eyes flash a brilliant yellow. "What is it about *Alice in Wonderland* that you love so much?"

Her mouth widens in a Cheshire smile. She shows her approval to the question by taking one of her hands exploring around my crotch. "I love how crazy it is," she says. The place is loud, but my attention is focused on her.

"It's nonsense," she continues, "it's lunacy. It's hallucinations and violence. It's everything I wish life was, but isn't. Unless.."

"Unless what?"

"Unless you're here!" she practically shouts. "This is the closest place I've found to Wonderland."

Her hand finally finds my erection. She smiles wide and brings her mouth close to my ear again. Her breath, hot and wet, makes me close my eyes. "Let's go somewhere private."

I can feel the eyes of the other people around us staring as she takes me out of the roped off area, through a collection of unused couches, to the end of the massive warehouse containing the party. She opens a hidden door.

There's a dim hallway lit in red with a dozen doors on either side. Some kind of sleeping quarters. I hear random sounds from various rooms, hard to pinpoint. She settles on one door and then leads me inside.

The room is small, but lushly furnished. A warm looking carpet, a mirror, and a bed. It doesn't look like much, but I don't have a chance to survey it. Jaz spins me around and kisses me. My hands reach for her body and find all the places I sought to explore earlier in the day. She's naked in a flash. I'm clumsier and almost fall once or twice. She laughs in a sweet kind of way.

The rest of the night is a blur. The drugs help me last a long time. When it's over, I collapse in a heap of sweat and labored breathe. I drift off . . .

When I wake up, Jaz is getting dressed. My vision is still blurry and I can feel aches and pains in places I hadn't used in a while.

"Hey," I tell her.

She doesn't turn to face me right away. She finishes getting dressed and sits on the one chair in the small space. Her face, so full of light yesterday, is dark. Her lips dip in a frown and her eyes are an ominous black.

"I'm sorry," she says.

Just then the door bolts open and two large tattooed guys burst in and go straight for me. One of them grabs me and pulls me out of the bed, naked, and then out of the room.

"HEY!" I scream.

I look at Jaz, but she's turned away. The guy holding me uses one of his massive hands to cover my mouth and stifle my screams. The other brute has all of my clothes.

They lead me down the hallway. Last night it seemed long and endless and full of possibilities, but this morning it's short and ends in a simple door, framed by light.

Sunlight.

"No," I whisper, "please."

The guy holding me pushes his hand further against my mouth. The other guy is rifling through my pants until he finds my keys. My car. My house. He smiles and nods and the bigger brute pushes me towards the door. He kicks it open.

And then I'm outside. The sun is an oven and I'm a raw chicken. I can feel my eyebrows burning. My skin roasts in seconds, sizzling. I can't breathe. I fall to my knees, the world dipping into black.

I think about Murphy. I hope they remember to refill his water.

It's so hot these days.

But My Heart Keeps Watching

I built my father out of bones.

There are photos of him all over our house. I know what he looked like on his wedding day, on the beach with his shirt off, on a boat with my mother with wind in their hair, and holding a baby version of me, his smile as big as my tiny head.

On Sundays, we went to the cemetery to pay our respects. His grave was alone at the top of a hill. Most days my mother is fine, sad but functioning, but on Sundays she's a mess. She cries and cries. She doesn't remember to make me lunch or dinner.

I asked her once, years after my father had passed, "Mom, why are so sad?" And she said, "Because my heart is broken."

The next day at school, I built her a paper-mache heart, painted it red and purple, her favorite colors, and gave it to her at night. I removed the gears from a clock and inserted it into the heart so that it looked like it was beating. I said to my mother, "I made you a new heart."

She laughed and patted my head and said, "You're sweet, Rose."

But I wasn't trying to be funny. I was being serious. I don't know what I wanted her to do, but it definitely wasn't laugh. I started crying and rushed to my room. I slammed the door so hard, it cracked a little.

*

My only memory of my father is when he used to take me to the city to visit the Museum of Natural History. He loved the history and we both loved the taxidermy.

The dinosaurs were my father's favorite. We stood in front of the massive skeleton of the Tyrannosaur for what felt like hours. I could see he wanted to reach out to touch the elegant bones.

I asked him, after a while, "How do they know how it all fits?"

My father looked at me with a strange expression.

"Like," I said, "No one has ever seen a T-Rex, right? So how do they know what it looks like?"

He smiled and pinched my cheek. "Bones are magic, Rosie," he said. He was the only person who called me Rosie. Then we went back to staring at the bones and I wondered what life was like millions of years ago when the world was young.

*

One day I went to the cemetery on my own. I snuck out of school during lunch and made sure no one was following me. I thought I heard someone call out to me as I was getting on my bike, but the sound of the wind drowned it out.

I rode through the deserted daytime streets towards the rolling hills of the cemetery. I stood over my father's grave for awhile. Then, as if he said something to set me off, I started cursing and punching at the ground. I shouted, "Why did you leave? Why did you make her sad?"

I started digging with my hands and crying. I didn't know what had come over me.

I made a decent size hole in the earth by the time the sirens approached the hill. Truant officers rushed out of the car and ran towards me. They were angry.

Later, my mom came to get me from school. I saw her in the principal's office crying. I was confused, because it wasn't Sunday. Every once in a while the door would open and I would hear her say something like, "She's acting out . . ."

*

After that day, everyone at school started treating me different. The other kids whispered as I passed them in the halls and the teachers talked slowly to me like I was dumb. The school suggested counseling and though it was expensive, my mom agreed. She took an extra shift at the hospital to pay for it and was home even less.

I spent more and more time alone. My mother asked other parents to drive me and pick me up from school. I'd come home and there would be dinner on the kitchen table, usually some drive-thru, and I would hear the TV on in her bedroom. I was never sure if she was asleep or at work. The red and purple heart was in the middle of a stack of forgotten mail in the corner of our kitchen. I listened to the tired ticks of the gears as I ate cold hamburgers.

For my plan to work, I needed help. I stalked a group of boys who hung out under a Banyan tree across from the soccer field. They played games out of their parent's old D&D books. I guess the new editions were too expensive. I coaxed a couple of them to the nearby bleachers and traded phone numbers.

I needed to get my hands on my father's remains. I wasn't sure why. I felt the pull of it when I was at his grave. It was like a vision. I had to see it through.

I spent the rest of the night texting.

*

The boys told me over Messenger how it went down.

Three boys met up near the cemetery. They had stolen shovels and pick axes from their high school maintenance sheds. There was night-time security in the area so one of them was lookout on an adjoining hill while the other two crept towards my father's grave. They had their cellphones on continuous three way conference call like some kind of away team mission in *Star Trek*.

Digging did not go well. The guys were weak and afraid. They told me they psyched themselves up thinking this was a morbid video game. They counted each shovel full as a point and kept a tally in their heads. They didn't even consider the crime they were committing.

After a few tense hours, where once a security guard in a golf cart rolled by but didn't see them, they had the casket uncovered. The two boys tied rags around their noses and mouths like they'd seen in the movies and opened the casket. They wouldn't tell me what it looked like inside except it was "gross."

I only needed a few bones for my project. They packed those in a duffel bag and left it at the lip of the hole. Then they went about refilling it. One of the boys almost collapsed and so he switched places with the lookout. They made it home before their parent's phone alarms went off.

One of them sent me a message: "It's done. Now, you're turn. Send us pics!"

I googled some leaked nudes of movie stars and sent them the images with the heads cropped off.

Boys are so dumb.

✳

The next morning, I picked up the duffel bag from behind a pile of garbage in the grassy field between the middle and high schools. I slung it over my shoulder and went straight home. I kept checking behind me as if I was being followed, but no one was there.

My father had used our garage as a work room. I remember it being so tidy and organized. He used to tinker with model airplanes and computers. After he passed, my mother never liked going in there. She had me bring boxes of junk in there every few months. There were so many now, they reached the low ceiling and blocked the lightbulbs. It was dark as a grave in there.

Over the last week, I had made some space between the boxes and uncovered my father's old steel table and tool bench. I laid the duffel bag on the table and turned on a desk lamp.

The boys had done well and brought me the handful of bones I needed. I connected them with pieces of copper and hard silver wiring. It looked like a stick figure of a person.

From below the table, I pulled out two shoe boxes covered in dirt. These I had unearthed myself from our backyard. They were the bones of dead pets from my early childhood, a bird, a cat. I don't know why my pets kept dying. Maybe that's just what pets do. Each of the shoe boxes had the name of the pet drawn on the top with crayons and markers but the letters were faded and I didn't remember their names.

I removed the lids from the boxes and carefully picked up a few of the skeleton remains and placed them on the table.

I worked slow and steady to get the pieces fused together. When I was done, the shape reminded me of a monkey, a kind of miniature human cousin. I used the skull of a cat as the head and the tiny stick bones of the bird to create fingers and toes. I threaded fishing wire between the larger human bones and the smaller animal bones to keep them together.

When I was done, I stepped away from the table and looked proudly on my creation. I had a fleeting thought that someone, like my mother, might see this and think it's a grisly scene of violence and murder. They would ship me off to an insane asylum with a name like *Shady Branches*. But to me, it was beautiful. It was pieces of my past all put together.

I reached into one of the drawers of the work table where I had hidden a folder of photographs. I didn't remove any of the pictures from the house. I snapped photos of them with my phone and then printed those out. The photos, once small enough to fit in a frame, looked grainy and weird when printed to fit on a page, but it was good enough. I placed the pictures of my father all around the bones.

Now, for the final touch.

I wasn't sure what technique was going to work, so I decided to employ them all. I researched countless rites and rituals on YouTube and sent links to my phone. I bought incense from a rank smelling shop downtown and chicken guts from a butcher a few doors away. I brought them all back to the garage. Each night, I worked myself into a sweaty mess as I tried to coax my father's soul back from the dead. I did rain dances and spun dreidels and even tried rake.

After a while, I gave up. I laid down amongst the beads and the sand and painted feathers and tried to sleep. I closed my eyes and after a moment, I heard a stirring like wind. I looked around to see if there were any open windows or doors. I heard it again, a rustle.

I leaped to my feet and looked at the skeleton on the table. When it didn't move, my heart sank. And then one of the arms lifted. Then another. It pulled itself off the table like an awakening zombie. It stood on the table, barely two feet, with its stick figure body and tiny cat skull. It looked at me and, amazingly, a voice came out of the bones.

"Rosie?" it said.

I couldn't speak.

The tiny skull took in the room and then looked down at its strange body. When it spoke again, I recognized the voice, the deep tones of my father.

"What am I doing here?" it asked me. "I don't remember.." There was sadness in his voice, a profound confusion.

I took a step towards it and extended an open palm like I might greet an alien visitor.

"It's okay," I said, "I'm here. You're back."

*

We went everywhere together.

He spent most of the day in my backpack, which I kept perched on one shoulder. He would whisper jokes or words of encouragement to me during the school day. Sometimes I'd laugh in the middle of a quiet moment in class and the teacher and the other kids would just look at me and shake their heads.

A couple of weeks later, one of the boys who dug up his bones tried to talk to me during lunch. His name was Travis and he wore skinny jeans and had a flop of unwashed brown hair that covered his eyes. He asked me some questions but I couldn't pay attention because my father became agitated as soon as Travis came close to me. He started banging on my shoulder through the backpack.

"I, uh," ouch! "I have to go," I said and rushed out of the lunch room. I was hungry the rest of the day.

Later, I went under the bleachers by the football field and moved my backpack to the floor and unzipped the top. My father's cat skull head peered up at me.

"Why did you do that?" I asked him.

"I don't trust that boy," said my father's bones.

"He's nice," I said but I dropped it. I didn't want to argue with my best friend.

That night, we watched TV together in the living room. My mom was at the hospital so my father laid on top of me on the couch. He liked to put his head to my chest and listen to my heartbeat. He said it made him feel human.

My phone let out an R2-D2 series of bleeps. It was Travis, texting me. He was asking me out on a date!

"Whoa," I said.

My father looked up. "What is it?"

"Uh, nothing. No one." I put the phone away and covered my mouth so he wouldn't see my smile.

*

The next weekend, my mom was working a triple shift and would be out of the house from Friday morning to Sunday night. She left me some cash and made me promise to eat at least two meals a day and both of them cannot be pizza.

I texted Travis and told him the coast was clear for him to drop by that evening. I just needed to figure out something to do with my dad.

My father was one of those old guys who could spend all day watching war documentaries on the history channel. I placated him at first after his reincarnation in bone form. I would watch endless hours of commentary and grainy footage about World War 2 and reenactments of civil war battles.

On the Friday afternoon after school, mid-way through a documentary on Hilter's breakfast habits, I got up and said, "I can't watch any more of this!"

His tiny bone fingers pressed pause on the TV. "What do you mean?" he said.

"I just can't!" I said, exasperated. "You watch whatever you want, I'm going upstairs to read."

I left before he even had a chance to respond.

Once in my room, I went straight to my window where Travis waited, crouched in the shadows of my curved roof. I had never had a boy sneak up to my room before. It made my limbs tingle with excitement.

"Hey," he said when I opened the window.

"Shhh!" I said and gestured for him to come in.

His expression was confused. "I thought you said your mom wasn't home."

I shrugged and thought quickly. "She still hired a babysitter!" I said with a sigh. "She's watching TV downstairs. We have to be quiet."

"Okay," said Travis with a smile.

He sat on my bed and looked around at all my posters and dolls, remnants from my not so long ago childhood.

"Cool room," he said and then patted the bed next to him.

I sat down, close but not too close, and said, "So, are you—"

He reached over and kissed me. It was short, dry, with a question mark at the end.

I nodded for him to continue and then he put one warm hand around the curve of my jaw and laid another long kiss on my lips. It was my first real kiss so I wasn't sure what to do, but he went slowly and we took a few breaks to breathe.

After a few wonderful minutes, his hands went wandering on my back and down to the hem of my blouse. He tried a few times to lift my shirt up to my chin, but I quickly clasped his hand in mine and stopped him.

He released his lips from mine and said, in a whisper, "Come on, Rose. Let me see them."

He tried again to lift up my shirt and I pushed back away from him. He looked surprised.

"Come on!" he said. "I knew the pic you sent was fake! If it wasn't, you'd show them to me."

He reached out again and I slapped away his hands. "No!" I shouted.

Just then, the door to my room burst open and my father, a diminutive skeleton of contrasting bone sizes, stood like a protective dog at my door.

My father's tone was all daggers. "You leave her alone!"

Travis' face was scrunched in disgust. "What the hell is that?" he said.

My father leaped like a long jumper from the doorway right onto the bed. He tackled Travis and both fell to the ground in a mess of limbs. They looked like they were wrestling, throwing each other on the ground and then back on top of the other.

"Get off me!" said Travis and he used two palms to shove my father back across the room.

Travis scrambled to his feet and rushed out of my bedroom. My father looked proud. He nodded at me and said, "You're welcome." I wasn't sure what to say.

✳

Word of the incident spread quickly through the town, as one might expect. Travis did not stay quiet. His report to his friends via text ended up on Facebook. From Facebook it went to Twitter, Twitter to Instagram, Instagram to Snapchat. After that, it left the ether of cyberspace and ended up in the real world in the form of phone calls to my mother.

My phone rang while I was eating cereal. It was my mom. She never called me while on shift. Occasionally she would text a "Doing OK?" but that was the usual limit of her communication. I swallowed a spoonful of Cheerios and picked up the phone.

"Yeah?" I said.

Her voice was already agitated, excessively punctuated. "Rose! I just got The. Strangest. Call. Do you have some kind of pet? It attacked a boy? Why was there a boy in the house? What is going on with you!"

I put the phone down without saying a word. As I put on my coat and shoes, I could hear my mom continuing to have a one way conversation with herself.

"Well? Well?" she said. "I swear, if you . . ."

I stopped listening.

My father was sleeping in the living room. I picked him up and put him in my backpack and left the house.

Outside, the morning was thick with fog. It was like it had been raining all night and suddenly someone pressed PAUSE and the rain just stopped and waited for input. The streets were slick wet and empty. I rode my bike, my hands gripped hard on the bars, back to where all this started, the cemetery and the gravestone atop a lonely hill.

My father was silent during the trip, a rarity. Usually he rattled off facts and advice as if it was nothing. He knew.

At the base of the hill, I stepped off my bike and let it fall to the ground. I crouched and swung my backpack in front of me. My father, all two and half feet of him, crawled out of the bag and climbed on top of me. He clutched my chest like a baby.

I walked him up the hill to his grave. I leaned down and he released his grip on me. He laid down on the grass and looked at me with hollow eye sockets that still somehow looked sad.

"Rosie?" he said.

"Yeah?"

"Can I hear it one more time?"

"Sure."

I got down on my knees and leaned my chest towards him. He put one side of his tiny skull against my chest. I could feel my heartbeat reverberate his bone body.

He leaned back, satisfied. "It's strong."

"No," I said. "It's broken."

Halfway Down the Hole

There's a ghost in the car.

It speaks in silence. It fills the holes of conversation. It is absence, as deep as a well, as black and cold as a December night.

I can see it in your eyes. You're thinking of him, too. I remind you of him, and you, me. We don't look at the backseat. We can't bear to see his sad, lifeless, eyes. His body so bright it's blue. His arms rest lazily on our headrests. Like a dog, he yearns for our attention.

If only one of us would say something, something funny or witty preferably, the memory might erase itself. Escape into the void, like so many forlorn thoughts and scraps of dreams. If only he would just go away!

I reach for the volume knob on the dashboard. A cranky, grating, guitar rises in anger. But it doesn't fill up the hole. There's still a mark, barely visible, but there if you know where to look, like the shadow of ink beneath a weak spread of whiteout.

*

We're brothers without the blood, you and me.

When our parents married, we were like hatching chicks, just beginning to understand the world. You're older by six years so our relationship, at first, was strained and distant. But then we merged as I got older. I don't know if I aged too fast or you too slowly, but it was like we were both reading the same book and somehow ended up at the same chapter and now were free to discuss characters and references and narrative possibilities. Our lives (the stuff that makes up life: likes, dislikes, favorite foods, movies, TV shows) melded together like lovers after a night of passion.

Remember that day we went to the movies? Paid for one ticket and saw four movies? Marathon-runners in dim shadows. The soles of our shoes sticky from popcorn oil. Our eyes glazed and dark-tinted.

What happened to us?

*

Oh, right.
Death.
Death erases. Death creates fissures. Death destroys.
But it didn't have to be this way, did it? Why did we let money and greed get in the way of family? How does that happen?
When he died, he took us with him, halfway down the hole, like Hamlet jumping into Ophelia's grave.
I can't believe he would have wanted it this way.

*

We arrive at our destination: The Aquarium.
He loved fish, so we decide to come here on the anniversary. Do you remember that huge tank we had in the old house, with the different habitat zones, and the three-dozen fish? Angelfish and transparent fish and whiskered-old-man-fish all living in peaceful, utopic, harmony.
The first exhibit upon entering the aquarium is a massive kelp tank. Tentacles of fleshy green sway like trees in a spiraling tornado. They fall and dip and almost seem to collapse until another breathe of unnatural current picks them up and then they're dancing again. It's hypnotic. Sharing the tank are fish the hundreds of colors of flowers. They float with the currents, drunk with laziness.
Darkened halls branch out from the tank. They look like vague choices in a dream. The Jolly Jellyfish to the left, the Mysterious Sea-Floor to the right, and in the center—we're already gravitating towards it, the safe route—The Monsters.
The tank is the size of an IMAX screen. It's empty of plant life and decoration but the monstrous fish still crowd each other for room. Tunas half the size of automobiles, benign sharks as quick and sly as stray cats, and shy stingrays hug the ground. There's stadium seating, but we stand inches from the tank, like disobedient children in front of the TV.

In the glassy, fish-eye, reflection, the two of us stand together but a space apart. Faintly, watery, I can see him standing between us.

✱

It was only after the funeral that the rift began.

There was a chapter break between one day and the next. A bright, optimistic chapter (despite the hospital scenes) followed by a dark, wounded, little brother of a chapter.

It was like a war. Rather, a battle for scraps. Between my mother and yours, and us in the middle, victims. Watch for stray bullets.

After a while, after the dust and pain had cleared, we got together in secret. I don't remember how it started. Did you call me, or did I call you? Are we betrayers? Or loyalists?

✱

When we step outside, it's raining. The droplets fall in wide tear-shaped bombs that explode noisily upon the concrete.

We're in no hurry to return to the car and the ghost. We sit on an uncomfortable bench with a roof and chain-smoke cigarettes. Unsupervised children slosh around in puddles and shriek at each other. Parents giggle. Couples clutch each other's arms and look lovingly in each other's eyes.

The weight of it all makes me sad. Maybe it's the memories. The brilliant past, so full of light and color and humor, the somber, slow, secretive present, and the dim future, wet and blurry.

I blurt out, "Why do we do this to ourselves?"

You look at me like I'm old and senile. "Huh?"

"This," I shout, waving an arm, indicating everything. "What do we hope to gain? He's following us. He's crushing us." I choke down a tear. "And I don't know how to let him go."

"Relax, man," you say, speaking soft and sage-like. Like the real flesh and blood older brother I always wished you'd be. "This won't last forever, this pain. Life goes on."

Platitudes. False hope. I'm offended.

"Bullshit!" I shout. "Look at us." Sad, sorry, sacks of flesh compared to the children so overflowing with life, I mean. (But I can't seem to say.) "Life doesn't go on. Life stops. It freezes. Here, right now, in this place and time, it just plain stops. Why are we still holding on?"

I'm crying now. Rain and tears everywhere. I can feel a tightness on my heart and my throat is scratchy from smoke.

"Life goes on," you repeat. More to yourself than to me. You look away and I know this will be the last time we ever see each other.

*

On the way back, we don't listen to music. We let the absence fill us, in search of answers. Answers in the darkness: in the blank stare of endings, in the emptiness of black screens and empty pages. It fills the little car until we can barely breathe.

In the backseat, the ghost lies down, closes his eyes, and waits.

Never Stop Moving

I thought we'd be safe underground. I watched through the back window of the subway car as the station fades, bright light replaced by tunnels and my darkened, haggard, reflection. My sister heaved on a nearby seat. She clutched her bags as if someone might try to steal them again.

"Bastards," she said under her breath.

There were four of them, younger than us, hoodlums from Harlem or the L.E.S. They found us camping in a rarely used tunnel connecting two subway lines. At first they wanted to steal our stuff then they saw my sister and had *other* ideas. I was able to bribe them with our meager savings, forty dollars worth of singles and coins. They walked away, smiling. We ran like crazy in case they changed their minds.

This was not the first incident. We've been trying our luck in the city, sleeping in squatter hotels and trying to fit in with other homeless teens. They look at us, white kids from Riverdale, and they see targets.

I finally caught my breath and ran a hand through my dirty hair. I looked back at my sister.

"We need to get out of here."

✽

It wasn't that we were homeless, but rather *sans*-home. We had a home. It was in a quiet green area of the Bronx, on a U-shaped street surrounding a large patch of grass and trees. We walked by it, just to make sure it was still there.

It was a small house, pretty in an unassuming way. The red brick walls and white-trimmed windows looked like any ordinary house. There were two floors of bedrooms plus a converted basement that was our parent's room. There were hardwood floors once, but our parents couldn't sleep with so many kids' heavy footfalls so when I was about fourteen, they re-did the first floor in carpet. Footsteps whispered, but our voices never did. In our house, conversations were always loud.

We never locked the front door. With five children and a parade of bestfriends and girlfriends and boyfriends, it just made sense to hang a metaphorical sign that said "Welcome! Someone's Always Home." I don't even remember having a key.

Now, the doors were locked. The large windows that shone so much light into the living room were blind. What once overflowed with music and laughter was dark and silent.

We can only imagine what's going on in that house. Whatever it is, we know it has something to do with warm food, pillows and blankets, and the constant chatter of TV. Those simple comforts we took for granted, but when they're *taken*, it's the things you miss the most.

*

Survival was priority number one. As the older one by three years, that was my call. Food, water, shelter, those were the things I wanted to focus on.

My sister thought differently. She convinced me to go into the city where so many other young people were in a similar situation. She said we could find allies and learn how to survive, but all we found was drugs and violence.

Early on, we went to lawyers. We tried to clean up as best as we could in public bathrooms and knocked on doors in local offices. Sometimes the secretaries would just wrinkle their noses and kick us out before we even had a chance to speak. One time we met with an attorney, a large man with a yarmulke on his head. We told him our problem. We explained it as best as we could without crying, but as soon as he started asking us questions ("Was there a will?" "Do you have any documents supporting your side of the story?"), it was as if we closed our eyes for a second and as soon as we opened them, there was a glass wall between us and him and we couldn't hear anything he said after that. His lips moved but there was only silence and an impatient and angry expression we knew too well.

*

Back in the Bronx, we spent the night under a tree near the local fire station. I had this image—it struck me while hiding out from bored police officers looking for someone to harass—of fire trucks peeling out of the station and the big wide fire station doors open and welcoming. If the trucks were called out on a job and they left the station empty, we could sneak in and hide out somewhere.

Unfortunately, there were no calls on that night. We chose a spot not too close to the building where we might be caught and so we were more exposed to the elements. It was one of our worst nights. The rain relented every hour or so but came back after a few minutes stronger. My sister was shaking by the morning, her brown hair dark as soot, her clothes pasted to her. Her teeth chattered. We each slept with two blankets over our sleeping bags. I placed both of mine on top of her so that she looked like a pile of laundry.

It was morning, five or six maybe. The world was hazy and quiet, still a little too early for the hordes of commuters to embark on their day. I decided to let her sleep and I would scrounge for food.

I got up and shook like a dog to get the water out of my clothes.

I walked over to the fire station. They had those big tin garbage cans full of discarded food outside but someone had forgotten to close the lids so the rain had filled them. Even a dog wouldn't eat rain-soaked hamburger leftovers.

Against the back of the station, there was a covered shed with some lawn and garden tools near the trash cans. I went over there to see if there was anything worth stealing. And that's when I saw it.

Lying on an upside-down milk carton was a cream-colored expandable file folder. The front was unadorned with a name or a label, but it seemed familiar somehow.

I kneeled down in front of the milk carton and opened the file. The first thing I saw were faded sepia-colored photographs of old Jewish people. I picked up the first pictures, turned them around, and written on the back was the unmistakable handwriting of my father. Hebrew names I couldn't read. Dates from the 50's and 60's.

I didn't stop and think and wonder what the hell this could be about when I grabbed the next few pictures. There was my father as a child surrounded by his brothers and sisters, almost too many to count. My grandfather in his candy shop. The old house in a suburb of Tel Aviv, familiar trees and shapes reminding me of a long-ago trip.

    I quickly went to the next group of pictures. There *I* was, a baby, held by a young version of my dad. The next picture had a three year old me holding my baby sister in diapers. Her cheeks were red from crying. There was my mother and father together in what must have been their first apartment. The furniture looked massive, the walls covered in ugly silver wallpaper, and in the center, my original family, smiling.

    The next group of pictures had my half-sisters and half-brother, dozens and dozens of pictures of all of us, young and smiling. Even my father looked young, a full head of dark hair on his head. There were birthday cards filled with the word Love bundled in with the photos. At that point, I could barely see.

    I had been crying. Drops splashed on the old photographs and made some of those ancient colors run. My brain ran circles around itself.

    After the photographs were thick bundles of papers. I flipped through them quickly. There was forms and letters, some typed, some handwritten. Copies of bills, checks, transactions. The quality on some of the paper was old, the type blurry and hard to read. I saw my last name on almost every page.

    I heard a footstep and a muffled voice behind me. I grabbed the file in a hurry, dropping a photograph or two and then quickly bending over to pick them up. The voice grew louder. I rushed away from it, in the opposite direction of where my sister slept.

    I clutched the file to my chest and ran.

*

The sun had lost its way. Curious, it ventured in directions it usually would not and found itself swallowed by clouds. Dusk came early and I realized I had been gone all day.

    I rushed back to the tree by the fire station but my sister wasn't there. I stopped and took a long breath. She was going to be pissed.

    We had a backup plan, in case we ever got separated. I ran, the file tucked away in my backpack, to an outlying park near our neighborhood. After the baseball fields where I once played Little League, beyond the rotted concrete and stringless hoops of a single basketball court, there was a stretch of wilderness leading up to the Hudson river. Somewhere in there was an abandoned car, its mysterious origins the stuff of our imagination.

On the hood of the car, amidst the plants that poked through the engine, my sister sat with her face buried in her hands. At my footsteps, her face shot up. Her initial expression was frightened, understandable for a teenage girl alone in the woods, but once she saw me, her features softened. She exhaled loudly.

And then she got angry.

She leaped off the car and came at me. She shouted, "Where have you been?!" and began to hit me, *hard*, on my shoulders and chest. "I was worried sick! It's been hours. WHERE HAVE YOU BEEN?"

It didn't last long. A minute and a half into her outburst, she collapsed from exhaustion, her shouts replaced by tears.

"I was so worried," she whimpered.

"I'm sorry," was all I could say. "I was . . . thinking."

She was still on the floor, weak from lack of food and crying. I got on my knees and held both her hands.

"I'm so sorry, M." I let go of her hands and swung my backpack between us. I unzipped it. My sister's watery eyes looked at me, hopeful. She probably thought I had a sandwich. I pulled the file out, photographs and papers poking out of the sides, and handed it to her. She opened it and started looking at it slowly, wordlessly.

When we spoke now, it was in low tones like we were in a synagogue.

"I was trying to figure out what to do with this."

"Who gave this to you?"

"I found it."

"You *found* it?"

"Yes."

Silence, but for the slow shuffle of paper. Birds chirped in the distance and a lonely frog sang to the trees. There was just enough light for her to see the shapes of the photographs and to read some of the words in the papers. We would have to leave soon, before it became dangerous out here.

She looked up at me after a while. "This is a gift," she whispered, almost too low for me to hear. Her face brightened for the first time since our father died. "This is our way out."

If she had the strength, I think she would have started dancing.

"We have to go," I said. "It's getting dark."

*

I wasn't in a great place at the beginning of the Worst Week and things only got worse as the days went on. It was fall and I had already gotten the flu. It took me awhile to recover and even then a nagging cough wouldn't let go. Plus my "year" at community college had stretched to two and I became increasingly isolated among the Black and Spanish packs of young adults.

It was with that heavy-laden heart that I came home one day to the news that my father was gone, dead in a car accident on the Brooklyn-Queens Expressway, DOA on the BQE. I don't remember my exact reaction. In fact, those few days after I found out are foggy, perhaps because of the drugs and alcohol, perhaps because my brain just couldn't really handle it and tried to push it all the way down into my low subconscious, never to be remembered.

I recall waking up one morning on my sister's bedroom floor. We had downed a bottle of Sky the previous night while listening to Boards of Canada albums. Books and photo albums were strewn around the room, damp from shed tears. We had pulled photos out and tried to remember those precious good times. Most of the photos were now face-down on the carpet.

My sister snored with some thin sheets around her ankles. I pulled a heavy blanket from the floor and placed it on top of her. She stirred, but did not wake.

I stepped out of the room and walked down the hallway to the kitchen for some coffee and a much-needed hangover breakfast.

In the kitchen was a bevy of activity and voices. My foggy brain took a moment to process it. My half-siblings were crowded around a small table while my stepmother looked on from the counter, typical arms crossed and face tight and emotionless. The smell of cigarettes was potent. My siblings, all highschoolers, were giggling and laughing.

They didn't notice me. I didn't expect us all to be mourning for the rest of our lives, but this was days after the funeral and these kids had moved on. They were his children too!

My blood started boiling and the synapses in my brain fired like rockets. I felt like I had just drunk my coffee. But then I stopped myself. I realized I had been shaking and maybe I was just jumping to conclusions. I was too hungover to process anything for real.

I kept my eyes on the tile floor and went straight for the coffee machine. They had not left me anything so I went through the sleepy motions of making a few cups worth. Nobody said 'Good Morning.'

My stepmother waited till I drank my first sip. I'll never forget what she said.

"I want you and your sister to start packing your things today. I expect you to be out of house completely by the evening."

Now I really started wondering if I was having a nightmare. "What are you talking about?" I asked her. "This is our home."

"No. This is my home now." Her voice was so level, her face only showing that constant, impatient, disapproving scowl. Her arms were so tightly crossed, I could almost hear the pressure. She spoke quickly. "Your father left no will. I've been to a lawyer and already have the paperwork claiming that everything that belonged to him is now mine. And that includes this house. And you are not welcome here any longer."

Shock turned to anger. "Are you insane?" I said. "This is our house. Our *family's* house. How can you do this less than a week after he's gone? How can you live with yourself after kicking out your own stepchildren?"

Her calm broke and her voice rose to a shriek. She flung her cigarette at the wall near my face. I almost wanted to cover my ears so that they wouldn't be shattered by that voice. "Your father only loved you and your sister! He didn't want you to leave this house even though you're both too *old* and *spoiled* to be here. My children deserve the space. My children deserve this house more than you! This house is mine and I want you OUT!"

I turned to my half-siblings for some hint of compassion or remorse, but they turned away. None of them looked me in the eye.

It occurred to me then that our family was not very strong if it could be shattered so easily.

*

My sister's been staring at the file for hours. It's late at night, two or three o'clock in the morning.

We found shelter from the rain in a garage of a large condo building. Most of these buildings have back doors for residents to walk their dogs. So many people came in and out, they rarely locked the door. We sneaked in around 9 P. M., and found a spot in a dark corner. I dragged a gray, dust-covered, wrap from a sports car and hung it up against a corner as if we were building a fort. We lit some candles, unrolled our sleeping bags, and tried to sleep.

At least, I did. She went straight for the file, putting the pictures aside and laying out the paperwork in stacks. She read silently, but her lips smacked and the occasional intake of breath indicated shock or awe. I watched and tried to doze off, but my body became too awake, too frightened and too freaked out because of the file.

I asked my sister, "Where do you think it came from?"

She shook her head. "I don't know," and went back to reading.

Ten minutes later: "I wonder if it was one of *them*."

She snorted. "Hardly."

But I thought about that for a few minutes. My half-siblings, the same shade of blood rushing through our veins, would one of them smuggle something out of the fortress of silence in a clandestine attempt to help my sister and I? I'd like to think it was possible. But then I remember those turned-away faces in the kitchen and think otherwise. The names and faces of my once-siblings are waning, as thin and weak as smoke from a forgotten cigarette.

"Maybe it was him."

My sister stopped reading and looked at me for the first time all evening. "What the hell are you talking about? He's gone . . . he's dead."

"I *know*. But maybe life isn't that clear cut. Maybe there's still a chance that our father was trying to help us . . ."

"No." Her words were sharp, each one tipped like a knifepoint. "There's no one trying to help us. There's just us. And this." She held the file like it was holy. "This is our savior. Tomorrow morning we can go back to one of those lawyers, and do what we've wanted to do since that bitch kicked us out of the house. We fight back."

Her usually stoic expression turned to a mean grimace. She was full of fire. Me, I felt waterlogged and exhausted.

"Tomorrow morning," she went on, "we're going to clean ourselves up and go back to that attorney. The fat one with the *kippa*. We have everything we need to mount a case against her. From what I've gathered from the file, she—"

"Wait a second," I said. "Isn't he going to ask where we got these papers? What are we going to say?"

She didn't answer for a minute. Then, "We stole it. We knew where our stepmother hid her important papers, so we broke into the house and stole them. It's plausible."

"I don't know . . ."

"Well, what the hell do you expect us to do, J? Sit on our asses with this information . . ."

"No, of course not. But we need to focus. Survival is the number one priority. Food, water, shelter, these are—"

"I'm *sick* of surviving. What about living? What about getting our life back?"

She started sobbing then, more out of exhaustion than anything else. She turned away from me.

We didn't speak anymore that night. We huddled into our sleeping bags on the hard concrete. Eventually the candles went out. I tried to sleep, but couldn't.

✳

My memories of my father are bleary like the morning, but I remember how he used to read to my sister and I before bed when we were young and shared a room.

He'd push a rocking chair between our beds and grab one of the many children's books from the wall, but that was just for show. He never read us what was in the books, but used those images and characters as inspirations for his own impromptu creations. He had wanted to be a writer, he admitted to me once, but didn't have the discipline. And like so many other things in his resigned life, he let it go.

But not during those bedtime story nights. After my mother left and before my stepmother arrived like an angry storm, those nights were quiet and safe.

My father tried his hand at parable: a story about a bear lost in the woods would turn into a lesson in "staying with the group" or some other advice. But there was one motif he loved to use the most.

"Close your eyes, kids," he whispered after a short story about a curious beetle. "Imagine you're standing in a river. It's warm and beautiful out, the rushing water feels great on your feet. You don't want to leave, so you don't. You stay in this amazing spot for days then weeks then months. But soon the seasons turn, its winter and the river has turned to ice. You're stuck. You realize you made a mistake. What was your mistake?" He paused, waiting for an answer. "You got comfortable and you stopped. Never stop learning or trying new things. Never stop moving."

Obviously, we didn't listen. Maybe my stepmother was right. We were too old to live at home. Maybe the stress of my stepmother's bitching and the weight of a full house caused my father's accident.

Maybe it was all my fault.

*

There's a place I like to go to think. Beyond the quiet streets of my tiny corner of the Bronx, beyond the undeveloped woods, beyond the forgotten car, there's a cliff-top overlooking train tracks and the green hills of New Jersey.

Sometime in the middle of the sleepless night, I picked up the various threads of the file left open by my sister, assembled them back together as much as I could, and put them in my backpack. I touched her hair while she slept, not sure if I ever would see her again.

I walked away from our little fort, tiptoeing so as not to wake her up, but I picked up speed once I got outside. By the time I reached the park, I was breathing heavy and sweating. I stopped to refill a water bottle. I felt a presence behind me. I smelled his scent, the way his skin clung to his aftershave, the faint aroma of his shampoo. I didn't want those aromas to go away, so I didn't turn around.

I looked forward into the woods and moved on until I reached the cliff side.

This place had been a comfort to me for as long as I could remember. There was beautiful endless water, a steady stream not polluted by nearby bridges, even the trains didn't bother me—their regularity was reassuring.

So it was here that I determined to discover the truth in the file. I grabbed some rocks and started spreading out the various papers and photographs. I secured them from the wind with rocks or my shoes or anything else I could find in the area. Soon enough, the ground looked like a corkboard in a police procedural TV show. Photographic evidence was grouped together by era, papers loosely tabbed in order of importance.

I still felt his presence, near me but not right next to me. I glanced sideways but saw nothing. But I knew he was there, hiding in the peripheral. What was he trying to show me?

I wanted to see what my sister saw. I wanted to understand how the file could help get our life back.

But I didn't see it. All I saw was the past, an optimistic past of the mundane, bank accounts and insurance, mortgage and car payments, some early documents about estate planning; nothing concrete.

I was crying again. It hurt so much, this past. It was everything I'd lost, everything I could have had if only my father was still alive.

I spun around quickly, hoping to surprise the ghost. I saw my father there, a transparent cloud, as tall as person, with a hazy face that looked like mine. He smiled his crooked smile at me, but his face betrayed his sadness.

That's when I got angry. I knew my sister was wrong, that there was nothing here for us. Even if any of these documents could help us, we couldn't afford a lawyer (we couldn't even afford lunch!) and did we really want years of legal wrangling just to end up exactly at the same place we were now, with nothing and no one?

No.

This file was not a gift, it was a curse. It was a reminder to her of what we lost. It had nothing to do with the present or the future. *It had to go.*

I went first for the photographs, the ones with baby versions of my siblings. I grabbed them and flung them into the Hudson River.

They scattered like frightened pigeons, filling the sky for a moment, and then gliding lazily into the water. Next, I went for a handful of papers.

"STOP!"

I turned to see her leaning on a tree, wheezing from running. "Stop, Jake. Please." She caught her breath and started moving towards me.

My face was a determined border guard. "One more step, and it goes into the river."

She didn't believe me so she kept me moving. I threw all the papers in my hands into the wind towards New Jersey.

"No!" she wailed. "What are you doing? Why are you doing this?"

"This isn't what we need," I said, pointing at the scattered paperwork. "This isn't some GetOutOfJailFree card. This is just more poison from our old life. We need to get *ourselves* back! We need to move on."

"NO! You're wrong. This is what we need to fight back. Without it, we are nothing!"

"We're already nothing. May, think about it. Do we have the resources we need? We don't even have a home address. We have nothing—"

"We have that file!"

"No," I said, "not anymore."

I started kicking the rocks that held the papers and photographs down. The wind was quick and my family history swirled around us in seconds. My father's ghost stood there with his life flapping around him, but he kept his eyes on me.

My sister lunged forward, desperate to grab anything, but the tears in her eyes and the weakness in her body didn't let her do much but fall to the floor, crying.

"I'm sorry," I said as the papers flew around us. Solemn faces of dead relatives looked at me as they descended into the river below. "I'm sorry," I said again, but I didn't really mean it.

I looked for my father's ghost but could only see fragments. The cloud dispersed as the wind picked up. Tendrils of white smoke unfurled towards the sky.

Moving up, moving on, always moving.

The Dying Disease

I always thought that when it rains that means someone died. Funerals need rain like they need flowers or a priest or a rabbi or an imam.

It rained a lot that summer.

*

The first things we noticed were the smell and the silence.

Tommy was making an omelet in our tiny kitchenette, the pan sizzling and cracking. He was humming some tune as he always does when cooking. I was strumming on a guitar on the ugliest couch in the world. We had woken up to an unpleasant odor from outside and closed the windows in our apartment. The place had A/C, but we couldn't afford to turn it on.

When Tommy shut off the stove, there was a kind of unpleasant quiet. It was noticeable. I looked up to find him already staring at me. Even with the windows closed, we should have heard more city noise. Car horns, hissing trucks, chattering people, the occasional shouted Spanish curse. Was it Sunday?

His omelet forgotten, Tommy joined me at the window. The glass was still wet from rain. I reached down to pull it open.

The smell hit us at the same time. Rotten eggs. Moldy vegetables. Old dog food.

New York, in summer, is known for its stench. Usually garbage left out on in the sun for too many days. Maybe a chemical fire in Queens.

This was different. This was *close*.

We sat on the couch and turned on the TV to local news. I hadn't watched local news since the last terrorist attack. I felt myself shiver at the thought of another.

Tommy's warm hand touched my own. He knew exactly what I was thinking. "It's okay," he said.

There was a disheveled man behind a news desk. He looked like he needed a coffee, a shave, and a drink.

He stopped mid-sentence to take a deep breath and started up again as if for our benefit.

"We don't know numbers yet, but police departments from all over the city are reporting massive numbers of sudden fatalities, in their homes, in their sleep, over the last few days. We don't know why. We don't know how many. We don't know…"

Here the man stopped again and reached his hand to wipe a tear from his eye.

"We don't know anything except they're dead. They're all dead."

*

We were musicians. Tommy was destined for Broadway and I was going to be the next Bowie. We came to New York on a dream and a few thousand dollars from our parents. We met online. I was from a small town, he was from an even smaller town.

I took the train. He took the bus. We met in Grand Central among the thousands of other people. It was so loud and so crowded, I'd never seen anything like it.

I remember he hugged me right away and it felt like we were old friends who hadn't seen each other in forever. We walked down the crowded New York streets, smiling at the girls and marveling at the buildings.

That felt like a long time ago, even though it wasn't.

On the morning after the epidemic made the news, everyone was freaked out. Social media fell silent and the streets were barren. We were afraid to go to sleep. Tommy and I finished all the coffee in the apartment in two days. Eventually, we slept and then woke up, a surprise every time. Is this what it feels like when the world ends?

Life continued, but in a crawl. Like fast-forwarding on the TV. It's still moving, but in such a fractured pace, you can't follow what's happening.

When the city put out a call for "Paid Volunteers" (no further details), we were among the first in line. We should have known what they needed, but I think we were still naive.

We became gravediggers.

*

It's like anything you do every day, it becomes familiar. Routine. Numb.

Another sealed apartment. Another quarantine sign. We used a crowbar to open the door and then slid patterned masks over our noses and mouth.

I will never be numb to that smell.

The apartment, like most in this small building on the West Side, was small and cluttered. Bookshelves overflowed, the kitchen had plastic shelving towers everywhere and the bedroom looked like a tornado hit a garage sale.

The corpse was an overweight woman on a lounger. She was in front of a large flat screen TV. Everything in the apartment was old except that flat screen.

Tommy and I held our breathe as we got her off the lounger and into a black bag on a stretcher.

In the beginning, they were concerned about the spread of disease. There was no cause of the sudden deaths, no discernible pattern, so they assumed an airborne contagion. We wore hazmat suits and layers of gloves to do our extractions. When no else died, the precautions were lifted.

Now we wore a mask and thin clear gloves as if we were working behind a deli counter.

It was grim work, but it needed to be done. The people who passed away deserved one last decent act. We owed them that. No mass graves. No trailers full of anonymous black bags.

"Let's do right by these folks," the Mayor told us in an airplane hangar in LaGuardia. There were hundreds of us "volunteers." Afterwards, he stood next to the CDC officials as they handed out the hazmat suits and was introduced to every one of us. He must have stood there for six hours.

The CDC studied the damn thing for months and no cause emerged. All they knew is that it was a global event. Billions of people passed away in their sleep, all over the planet. Half the population of the Earth.

They called it the Dying Disease.

*

Half the population.
    This wasn't the Sudden Departure. This wasn't Thanos.
    This was old fashioned death on a grand scale. It was like half of the world just decided to give up that night. Except we know they didn't. We know they wouldn't.
    Right?

*

We took turns driving. Today it was my turn.
    As usual, the city streets were quiet. There was graffiti everywhere, most of it about the end of the world. We were on our way upstate, to the makeshift cemeteries set up by the state.
    Outside the city the trees, like everything else, were dying. The leaves were turning brown and red and littered the floor like doll parts in a child's play room. Grey nimbus clouds threatened rain.
    Out of respect for the dead body in the van, we didn't listen to music. We barely talked. Tommy was chain smoking cigarettes, a new habit. I hated the smell, but what could I say? If he needed it to cope with all of this, if it helps even a little, he should do it.
    I joined the line of cars at the cemetery gates. A couple of hearses but mostly vans. When it was our turn to pull in, we drove down row after row of temporary markers with names and dates. I drove slow and it took forever before we got to an open space. Professional gravediggers were working a couple rows down, breaking the earth to create new graves.
    I pulled the van to the end of the lot. Tommy put out his cigarette in an already full ashtray in the dashboard.
    We began our work in a drizzle that became a torrent. The storm didn't last long, but it was enough to soak our clothes. By the end of it, our clothes were heavy and dirty and there was smears of green and black on our faces.
    Our final task was putting the wooden markers down. Names and dates. At the end, is that all that life is: A beginning and an end with a blurry middle section?

As is our habit, we took a full minute in front of the markers, silent, staring at the fresh plots and wondering who these people were. What was their favorite song? What did they like to watch on TV? Who did they love?

*

It started to get cold. We wore windbreakers and heavy pants. Then gloves and scarves and coats. It reminded me of the hazmat suits from the early days of our work. Layers between us and them, the bodies.

Endless bodies.

Every morning, the city texted us names and addresses. We went block by block. No days off, no weekends.

Occasionally we'd see another extraction team wheeling a stretcher out of a building or a townhouse. We exchanged no words, but a nod of understanding, of mutual compassion.

It weighed on us. Tommy didn't talk much these days. He cried himself to sleep. One night, I let myself into his room and into his bed. I held him for a long time.

After a while, I did more than just hold him. He initiated the first kiss and I kissed him back. I never felt anything for a man, but it was different now. Everything was different now. And it was Tommy. He needed me.

We held each other under layers of blankets as it snowed for days. No trucks would plow the snow. Big cities like New York became known around the world as Ghost Cities. Only a few bodgeas were still open. Everyone left to smaller towns to be around living people. The only people left in the city were us, the clean up crew.

The half dead.

*

One night, I held Tommy while we watched the sunrise. We didn't sleep much these days.

He wiped a tear from his right eye and said, "You know, I've never been in love. Isn't that pathetic?"

He did that sort of embarrassed laugh he does.

"I don't think it's pathetic," I told him. "Finding love is a lot about timing, you know?"

"Yeah, my timing sucks."

He snuggled a little closer to me and I expected him to say something sweet, but he didn't.

*

After a while, the texts from the city stopped. We'd get one body every few days. Those were long days. It was freezing outside and nothing was open anyway. Our musical instruments gathered dust in a corner. We stayed in. Made soup. Watched Netflix. Had sex. Got on each other's nerves. Sat in uncomfortable silence. I read. He paced and smoked.

Out of the blue, he said, "I'm going home."

I was wondering who would be the first to bring it up: moving. Out of the city. Like everyone else.

"Okay," I said. "I'll go with you."

"No."

"What do you mean, No?"

"I mean . . ." He lit another cigarette. "My parents, they wouldn't approve."

There was a couple of different layers of sting there. First of all, my parents were gone. Victims of the dying disease. His parents were alive. Second, what fucking decade is this?

"That sounds like bullshit," I said, not hiding my anger. "Sounds like you're scared."

I would have stormed out if it wasn't zero degrees outside and somehow colder in the hallways of our building. I got up to leave the room.

"You're right," he said. His hand pressed on my forearm. He was always warm. "It's not my parents. It's you. You and me."

"What the hell does that mean?"

He stepped away from me and exhaled a thin white cloud. "It's all this. Everything we've been doing. I'm never going to be able to look at you and not think about graves. And dead bodies." He sat down, tears welling in his eyes. "Doesn't it bother you?"

I sat beside him on our ugly couch. "Of course it does. But I'm hoping we can move past it. A couple of years, we can forget all this and eventually, be happy."

He buried his tear-stricken face in his hands. The lit end of his cigarette threatened to catch his hair on fire. "I don't think that's true. I don't think there's any happiness to be had. Not now, not in a couple of years." He sniffed back his tears and stood up. "You need to accept the fact that the world ended that morning. We're just ghosts. And ghosts don't get to be happy."

*

Let me clear up the mystery.

The world doesn't end in a bang or a whimper. It ends in silence.

It ends with a man sneaking out of an apartment early in the morning. Shuffling around, trying and failing to be quiet, slowly closing the door behind him as if I wouldn't hear it.

It ends in tears that fall like rain.

Young Man, Are You Lost?

"It's not enough," says the cashier behind the bulletproof glass. I'm gripping the bottle so tight it feels like it's mine already. I look over to the front door. It would be so easy to run. Then I look closer, above the doorway, to a tiny machine gun hidden in the frame. Don't let its size fool you. I've seen those things turn a Regular Man into a Holy Man.

I turn back to the cashier, a dark-skinned piece of work with crumbs in his bread. His T-shirt barely fits his massive stomach. I think, *This guy will sympathize. He knows what it's like to need something so bad it hurts.*

"It's all I got," I plead with him. On the tray between us are a few gnarled bills and some pennies.

The dark man gives me an even darker look. "Not enough," he repeats.

"Come on, Amir," I say, trying to get him on my level. "You know me. I come in here every day! I got my check coming at the end of the week. I just need something to get me through the night."

He nods to himself. Maybe he's considering my proposal, maybe he's going to give me a break, one soul to another. Then he smiles huge like a clown so I can see smears of chocolate on his teeth.

"Get out," he says.

"Come on, my friend!" I open my arms a wide, a universal gesture of peace.

It only angers him. "Get the fuck out or I call police," he says in broken English, waving an arm, shooing me away like a dog.

"Fine!" I shout. I grab my money from the tray and shove it into my jeans pocket.

I step outside into the cold night. There's a slight rain coming down. Headlights flash past on the street. The liquor store parking lot is deserted. Fluorescent lights from the nearby stores and motels buzz. I can feel the headache coming on. It starts small with a teeny hammering but will soon become a chainsaw.

Sober, bitter, and angry, I talk to myself. "Fucking immigrant piece of shit motherfucker. FUCK YOU!" I shout to the wind and the liquor store. "Taking shit from me! Just like everyone else!"

I'm not an alcoholic. I'm just in the middle of a multi-year bender and I'm not inclined to stop anytime soon. The trick is to keep going. Drink, smoke, snort, inject whatever you can get your hands on. That's how I survive. If you fall asleep, good, get your energy back up to start the cycle again. Food is only necessary at the tail end of a high. The *real* trick is to never come down.

It was going pretty good in that regard until that *motherfucker* got in the way.

I gotta get some money, obviously. There are ways, some more Kosher than others. There's robbing and stealing. But I've had problems with that in past. I'm not as fast as I use to be and if some punk kid or cop decides to give chase, I'll be ass-first in an alley in no time flat.

I used to run schemes on the tourists downtown. Back when there were tourists downtown.

I find a bench underneath a broken streetlight. There's a sign with a picture of a bus on it nearby. Buses haven't run through this part of the city in at least five, six years. There's a business idea! Start up some kind of van service, shuttling junkies and vagrants from one side of the ghetto to the other. I'd need a van and a driver's license. Or, at least, one of the two.

Some footsteps come up on me. I reach down to try to find my knife. It's usually in my front pocket. It takes a long moment but I grab it and swing around, some pennies dropping on the floor in the process.

An old man in a professor's tweed jacket, hat, and corduroy pants stands half in the shadows beside the bench. I breathe a sigh of relief. "Fool," I say, "I almost *killed* you!"

The geezer's voice is crackly like cereal, popping, losing words. "Young man," he says, "Are you lost?"

"Motherfucker," I spit back. "This is my town. I ain't lost."

I still have the knife gripped in one hand. That doesn't stop this crazy dinosaur from taking a step forward into the light. His skin is in worse shape than his voice. It's crumbled like discarded paper. Grey hair pokes out underneath his wide-brimmed hat and his face has hundreds of tiny pimples, some with long white hairs.

"No," he says, elongating the vowel. He has a speaker's voice, like a radio personality, a hint of an accent. "Not 'lost' geographically, but metaphysically. Do you know who you are? Do you know why you are here?"

I think about putting the knife away. This old dude's strange words are at least making my headache the *second* thing I'm thinking about right now.

"Maybe not," I say, "but who does? Who knows why they're here."

"I do. I can help you," he says. One step closer.

"Yeah?" I say, "You want to help me? Get me some booze and I'll be your best fucking friend."

The old hick shrugs, reaches into his jacket pocket, and pulls out a flask. Its polished silver looks clean, the cleanest thing I've seen in years. He twists the cap off with his thumb and hands it to me.

It could be poison. It could be turpentine mixed with sleeping pills and gasoline. I don't even sniff it first. I put the top to my lips and tip the flask back like its water and I'm dying in a desert.

The alcohol goes straight to my brain. It tastes like gin. After another two swigs, I'm feeling like myself again.

"I have more," says the old man. "I brew it myself. Would you like to see?"

I take another drink. It's either strong as hell or I'm thirsty as hell. I nod my agreement and reach a hand out to grip his shoulder.

"Lead the way, my man," I say. This guy's my hero. My own Alcoholic Guardian Angel.

As we walk in the opposite direction of the liquor store, he talks.

"My name is Dr. Peshe. I'm a psychologist by profession, but a bit of a Jack of Trades in practice. I dabble in pharmacology, astronomy, physics, thanatology, perfumery. Plant and animal husbandry. And homebrew alcohol, as you've already experienced." He looks back at me and smiles. His teeth are unnaturally white. Like what you would imagine the teeth of children would be like if they were never exposed to candy.

"Ah, here we are," he says. "Home Sweet."

His home is a boat secured to a wall with chains. There are no lakes or oceans nearby, only rivers and canals in this city. His boat is in one of these man-made passages, I look down and see only a few feet of water. The bottom of the boat is green with algae.

I lean over the side of the wall to look a little closer and feel my balance slipping.

The old man grabs my arm, tighter and stronger than I would have imagined, and pulls me away from the edge. When I look back at him in shock, he only smiles again.

"Careful there, young man," he says.

My head is swimming from whatever sweet substance was in that flask. I reach into my pocket for some more but find the flask missing.

The old man is holding it, its silver picking up the shine of the moon. "It's empty. But there's more inside."

Hungrily, I follow him over a creaky plank to the ship's hold. I have to crouch to enter the first rounded doorway.

I've been inside boats before, on tours of famous navy ships. Those were brightly lit and cleaned in military precision. By contrast, the inside of Peshe's boat is a hoarder's paradise. Dark and claustrophobic with cobwebs on every corner, trash on the floor, and an ever-present stench of cat piss. If there is light in these corridors, it's either half dead or blinking some form of SOS plea for help.

We arrive in the center hold of the boat. There are shelves lining every wall, all packed with jars adorned with labels and dates. Inside the jars are a multitude of liquids, some brown, others a frightening green. A few of the jars have brightly colored liquids inside.

There's a desk with a laptop and a messy display of wires that rise to the low ceiling and snake out across the room. Some couches stuffed with books and newspapers. At least two, no, three cats sleeping on top of piles of loose paper. A kitchenette, with a tiny fridge and an even smaller burner stove, is in the farthest corner.

"Please," he says, "Sit!"

There's only one chair, a faded red lounger, not drowning in clutter. It's dead center, facing one of the couches.

I take all this in with a mild sense of disgust, but it doesn't really affect my buzz. The doctor's shit is *gold* and I feel great.

I sit and lean back as much as I can in the old chair. "My man," I say, "You said something about a refill?"

"Ah, yes, of course," says the doctor, already fiddling with something or other. He shuffles over to one of the shelves and pushes aside some derelict newspaper to unveil a spigot connected to one of the jars. The liquid inside is a pale brown. He grabs a plastic cup from the floor and fills it.

He walks over to the center of the room to hand me the cup. Outside in the city he seemed to be frail, stepping slowly. Inside his lair he moves swift and confident.

"Drink up," he says and then sits down on the couch in front of me. He doesn't bother to move aside any of the clutter, just finds the perfect spot to sit his ass down. An ass-shaped space.

"Now," he says, "Young Man—"

"You don't need to keep calling me that," I say, barely though my first sip. "I have a name, you know. My folks called me Donald. You can call me Donny."

"Okay, Donny," he says. "Tell me about yourself. I heard you yelling in the parking lot. I assume you weren't always this way. What happened to you?"

"Naw, man," I say, "That wasn't me. I don't yell. I'm fine." I feel my thoughts ping pong back across my head. I almost start laughing at the thought of words like balls bouncing around my head.

"I know what I heard," Peshe says, suddenly serious. "I see what you are. I can see your past. You've had violence and pain in your life, probably associated with loss. Who did you lose?"

The balls in my brain stop in midair. They fall like someone just changed the level of gravity. I look at Peshe. He's looking less disheveled than before, like being home is enough to remake a man.

"My dad," I tell him. I put the cup to my lips to take another sip, then stop and put it back down. "My dad died years ago. He left me some cash, nothing huge but would have been enough to get my life in order. I had a wife, mortgage, and a kid in high school. But I never got the money. My brother and sister stole it from me. They worked together to rob me of my inheritance. I tried to fight them, spent every penny I had on lawyers. Then I lost my house. And then my wife left me. And my kid won't take my calls. And that, Doctor,"

I take my drink, downing it all in one shot, "is my fucking story. Nothing new. Shit like this happens all the time. I'm just the sucker this time around."

Peshe is standing next to me. He puts a hand on my shoulder. "It's okay, Donny," he says, "It's all okay."

The alcohol swims in my brain like an Olympian making laps. Back and forth across the pool of my mind, back and forth.

Back . . .

Forth . . .

I doze off.

When I wake up, my vision is blurry and my thoughts weighted down. I can't move. I can wiggle my fingers and move my torso a bit, but my arms and legs are clasped in place.

"What. The. Fuck."

"Ah," Peshe says, a beaming smile from his shining mouth. "Good morning. Or, actually good evening." He laughs at his own joke. I hate that.

"What the fuck is going on, old man?"

He is busy walking around me, playing with instruments or something I can't see.

"We're in the middle of an experiment. It's actually ground-breaking." He pulls a long tube in front of me. "I am going to extract your sins."

I feel a pricking in my arm. I look down to see a series of long clear tubes connected to my arm. Maybe seven or eight per arm. Peshe pulls a long needle out of the end of a new tube and sticks it into my arm.

"Goddamn it! Stop that."

"But why? This will only help." He moves around in front of me again. I'm tied up on the lounger with my feet up. Peshe gets very close to my face, almost straddling me on the bed. "You are full of sin, Donny. You are lost. I will help you. I will pull away those terrible thoughts that force you to drink."

With a grin, he tightens one of the straps. "You see, Donny, sin is power. It is all your craven thoughts and all the passion of your heart and your mind mixed together. It's the fuel in your fire and the burning in your gut. I can harness that power. I can massage it for new, productive purposes. You were just wasting it."

I try to push my way out of the grips but they're too tight. "Get away from me! Let me go!"

"No," he says, "not until you're cured."

He disappears behind me. I can feel that tiny bit of sobriety back in my head. It makes me angry. I scream some more obscenities at him, stringing together some choice curse words, throwing in some Arabic and Patois I've learned on the street. There's a loud cranking sound that begins behind me, like an ancient engine has been turned on. I can even smell the fumes.

And then the tubes start pulling into me. I look down to see my blood extracted at an obviously unhealthy speed. But it doesn't look like normal human blood. It's not red, but rather tinted in so many different colors, like black and green and orange. And it hurts like hell. Like he's drilling into my body and pulling out my organs in liquid form.

I scream, I think. Everything becomes hazy. I feel like the boat is moving, churning through rough waters.

I see Peshe standing in front of me, drinking from a clear glass cup. "Yesssssss," he snarls. "That's good!" He puts the cups to my lips and forces me to drink. It doesn't taste like alcohol. It tastes metallic like blood but mixed with some kind of sugar.

"How do your sins taste, Donny? Can you tell the difference between hate and greed? Between anger and lust?"

I have a brief moment of clarity when the room refocuses and I can hear the machine behind me and feel the slight sway of the boat. I look down, a huge mistake, and see the tubes still pulling rainbow colored blood from my veins.

Then I black out again.

When I come to, the sound of the motor behind me has subsided. There's only silence and the ever so slight crashing of waves against the ship's hull. My breath is coming out in ragged heaves like I've been exercising. My throat is dry and I need a drink, preferably water.

My vision is blurred and I feel lighter by twenty or thirty pounds. I'm still in the cluttered hold of the ship. The smell of stale urine is everywhere. A figure stands in front of me. It doesn't look like the doctor, but his clothes are familiar. He turns to me and leans in so close I can smell the alcohol on his breathe.

His skin is smooth, tinted brown. His eyes are black like mine. His teeth are bright white. He wears Peshe's tweed jacket but his face and body are different, leaner.

"You feel better?" says the man in Peshe's deep voice. "I know I certainly do!" He laughs, loud and boisterous. He stands up straight and stretches his arms and back.

"Yes, this will do." The doctor grips my leg like I'm his new toy. "Now, young man, shall we have more?"

Life in a Glasshouse

I miss the birds.

The seesaw rhythm of birdsong. The lifelong game of Marco Polo. Chirp. Are you there? Chirp. I'm here. Chirp. Are you still there?

My reverie is broken by a splash of plasma fire by my head. Everything speeds up to normal and I tighten my grip, one hand on a rope, the other clutching a scared kid.

"Hold on!" I shout and he grips my midsection a little harder. I pull the rope down just as the platform falls away underneath us.

I swing across the room like Tarzan minus the jungle. I'm in a cavernous cargo space, a tent city below. A group of angry thugs are chasing us, shooting wildly and shouting. There's a suspended walkway hanging from the ceiling. The rope swings us towards it, but we're not going fast enough, we lose momentum and swing back the way we came.

I curse and tighten my grip on the rope. The kid squeezes. I swing my legs this time and we pick up speed heading towards the walkway.

I zoom in. The world slows to a crawl. Sparkling beams of plasma fly by in slow motion. I reach with my free hand to the walkway. I grab and feel steel. I let go of the rope just as the world speeds up again and I've got two hands on the steel walkway now. The kid loses his grip on my middle, starts to slide down.

I reach down and grab him by the shirt. I pull him up, my arm screaming at me, until he grabs the platform with his own hands. Only then do I pull myself up and help him to his feet on the walkway. More angry splashes of fire from below.

"Come on!" I yell at him. We head towards a closed hatch. I click it open with a sensor in my arm. We bow our heads as we enter the quiet of the next room. He's breathing heavy even though I'm pretty sure I did most of the work.

"Now," I tell him between labored breathes. "You stay in your own town from now on, okay?"

"Yes, ma'am," he says. "Thank you, ma'am." And then runs off. Ma'am?

*

The hall in front of my shop is crowded with grifters and buskers. You could find anything in that place from prostitutes, drugs, subdermal enhancements, even Girl Scout cookies, twenty years past the expiration date. The lack of crunch isn't so bad. We're used to it.

Some of the regulars shout greetings at me.

"Yo D!"

"Hey Darcy! Check this out."

They're trying to get my attention because they want me to buy something. Normally I would, because I need to eat and also because they're my neighbors. But money is tight these days. I motion to my wrist and apologize.

I squeeze my way through the crowded thoroughfare to the metal door of my shop. I punch in a code and it slides open. Inside, it reeks of marijuana smell and motor oil. A head pokes out of a mess of wires and screens like a startled llama.

"Boss!" says Hurley, my friend and lone employee. "I *have* to show you something."

Before I can say anything, a dozen speakers in the cramped space wail at me. Incoming call. Hurley, nonchalant, picks up the non-lit end of his joint and takes a long puff.

"Put it out, man!" I shout at him. "Wait!" I take a long step towards him and motion for him to hand me the joint. The sirens continue. I take a puff. "Now put it out!" I tell him. "Idiot."

He grins at me.

I shake off some dust and dirt from my shirt. "Alright," I say, then louder for the computer to hear, "Answer."

A scruffy, dark-eyed face appears on the wall. Captain Duggart, police chief. His camera is tight on his face and huge from my perspective so I can see all the gray hairs mixed in with the black ones on his beard. Some kind of cake residue, too. His eyes are hollow and skin pale from lack of sun.

"Captain," I say, "are you taking your vitamins? You look paler than usual."

"Not the best way to start a conversation, Darcy," the cop says in a tired tone.

I slide some junk from a chair and sit down to remove my boots. "Yeah, well, I'm not one for ceremony." Then, with a smile: "Sir."

Duggart stares at something off screen. "Heard you took some fire this morning."

I brush a bit of burned leather off my jacket. "They missed."

"And the suspect? Where is he?"

"Ran off."

Off in the corner of my eye, I see Hurley hide a little more. Duggart turns his attention to me with the kind of expression I can only describe as "frustrated parent."

"He was supposed to be detained."

"He was just a kid."

"And?"

He breathes through his nose to calm himself. I continue, nonplussed, "I think he was framed. Didn't seem like the thieving type, if I'm being honest, sir. Maybe someone else did the stealing and blamed it on the kid. He ran off to hide in a neighboring town and got into more trouble. Could have had a body on your hands if I hadn't intervened and extracted him from the situation."

I smile at him. He doesn't look pleased.

"Darcy, I am forced to remind you, *again*, you are not police. You don't make decisions on who gets arrested. You had a job to do, which based on the fact we do not have a suspect to question regarding the crimes, means you failed. No payment."

He reaches for something offscreen.

"Wait, hold—"

The image blinks away.

"Shit," I say. I look at Hurley. I'm suddenly feeling tired. "You said you wanted to show me something?"

*

I pass some cash to Hurley's account and promise to deliver a real paycheck one of these days. He doesn't give me any shit about it, but

I know it's not easy. His "breakthrough" of the day was a new way to ping movements of suspects using the colony's heavily secure surveillance system.

"Assuming I can crack it," he said with such a proud smile, it was like he was holding his baby.

I take a walk down the thoroughfare. It's afterhours so the crowd is less overwhelming. There's still people about, as always, but there are a bits of calm, small clearings in the mess of cables and boxes and tubing that lines the walls and ceilings.

I miss the sky.

I can see it clearly if I close my eyes. As blue and startling as I'd ever seen. Wispy white clouds like paint strokes in the sky. The sound of silence, stillness.

Not here. Never here. That everpresent hum of machinery behind every wall stalks me like a bad boyfriend.

My short daydream is interrupted by a gruff guy pushing his way through the thoroughfare. Before he can collide with me and pass off whatever stink he's carrying, I zoom in, slow down the world, and slide away from him so by the time the world returns to normal speed, he's down the way and I'm inside a nearby bar.

This was my destination anyway. A drink and something to take my mind off the day. I order a straight whiskey, double, and sit at the bar. In front of me, behind the dusty bottles, is a wall of colony memorabilia, including signs from the early days. There's some post cards of various beach destinations taped to the dirty glass, ancient memories of an Earth that no longer exists.

Earth, at the beginning of the century, was in trouble. Climate change had created super storms and set a quarter of the world in flames. Governments, united for once at the global threat, rushed to find contingency plans in case our planet became unsustainable.

With limited options, they looked to the moon. Rockets, loaded with living spaces, made hundreds of trips until the surface of the moon looked like the stage setup for a multi-day music festival, after it was hit by a tornado. It took a while, but all of that raw material made its way underground, to the blank canvas of moon rock.

They had no idea what was going to happen.

After a few minutes of nursing my drink, a guy walks over and sits next to me. My immediate impression he's not bad looking and that's half the battle. Before the stranger can speak, my wrist beeps at me. I twist my arm so I can see my forearm and the built in screen in my skin. A message from Captain Duggart. A picture of a man with a Wanted sign below and a short but sweet bit of text from the old cop:

A chance to redeem yourself.

I finish my drink in a single swig and smile at the stranger. Maybe next time.

*

When the colony first started, it was separated by nationality. All the major countries of Earth participated in the planning and construction. The big countries grabbed the largest areas and smaller countries were relegated to off-the-beaten-path corridors and distant hallways. Each country even had a consulate inside their towns, back when everything was pre-planned and debated. Before everything went to shit Earthside.

I buzz Hurley as I leave the bar. His tiny visage appears on my forearm. Somehow, he looks more stoned than usual.

"Sorry to bug you," I tell him. There's a tiny micro-receiver in my ear so I can whisper and he can hear me and his voice comes through to me only. "Got a ping. Rush job." I take a breath. "American."

"Oh boy," he says. He moves to a computer terminal in his place. "Send me the digits."

I bring up Duggart's message and swipe it up to Hurley. Every mission sent to us has a corresponding case in the Police database, which is secure, but we have access. Hurley scans the file and then breaks down the salient points.

"Target is Leonard Jacobson. Retired Admiral, U.S. Army." Letters scroll through the reflection on his glasses. "Looks to be cozy with local mafia. Lots of coded transmissions. Never married, but has a long list of girlfriends." Hurley adjusts his glasses and looks at me through the screen. "You're his type."

I smirk. "I'm everyone's type. Where can we find Mr. Admiral tonight?"

Hurley takes another minute to look it up. "There's a party in one of the lofts. Jacobson's not on the guest list, but that's not a surprise. If he's out tonight, that's where he'll be." Hurley looks at me again. "But you'll need to change."

"Whatever," I tell him. I stop in front of a reflective strip on a wall. My reflection is blurry, but I've got my usual jumpsuit on underneath a brown leather jacket and black boots.

"It's a Patriot Party, Darcy. Fancy."

"No time to change," I tell him. "Duggart said it was an urgent catch."

"Can't you do your thing?"

"My thing?"

"Yeah, you know"—here Hurley dips his voice to a whisper as if someone can hear him—"your *power*."

I reach down to grab the zipper of my jumpsuit and pull it down below my chest.

"Better?" I ask him.

"You'll definitely make an impression."

"I always do."

*

Even as a child, back on Earth, I understood contrasting classes. I lived in an apartment building and played on concrete streets. I would ride my bike for ten minutes and end up on rolling hills of green fields, trees everywhere, and large brick houses that stood like monuments to money. I usually spun around and headed back to my block soon after.

I have that same uneasy feeling as I ride an elevator up to the lunar lofts. The architects built these, for whatever silly reason, with clear glass. Below, I can see the ramshackle streets and arcades of the towns. Hastily built shanties, always threatening to collapse, and overcrowded streets with clouds of steam and smoke.

Then a *whoosh* sound and the clatter of life below is replaced by silence and white, puritan walls. The American section of the Lunar colony is uncluttered and uncrowded.

The elevator stops and a group of guards greet me with plasma rifles up to my face.

"State your business!"

I take a step forward, the black barrel of two guns brushing against my cheeks. I think about how I can take them out. A quick zoom and I could get behind at least two of them, but four on one is difficult, even with, as Hurley put it, my "power."

"Relax, boys," I say, feigning nonchalance. "I'm an American. Check it." I reach for a pocket in my jumpsuit. The guards tense and lift their weapons higher. "Relax, guys. Seriously."

I take out a slim blue booklet and hand it to the head guard. He doesn't lower his weapon as he opens the booklet and stares at it.

"This looks fake," he says. "Birthdate is wrong."

I sigh and plan out my attack.

A voice from a few meters out calls out a warning, "Stand down!" it says and the guards lower their guns.

Striding in from the end of the corridor is a familiar figure. He's wearing all black, a few thin strips of gloss stand out against the matte of his pants and long sleeve shirt. He's got a badge at his hip and a scar running from his right eyebrow down to his neck.

Eric Tamer walks towards me and the guards part and grumble something and start to walk away.

"Hey Darcy," he says. "Been a while."

"Thanks for the assist, Eric. How's the face?"

He grimaces just a bit. "Hurts when I smile."

"If I recall, it could have been worse."

"If it wasn't for you," he says.

"I guess we're even now?" I tell him.

"Sure."

We walk for a minute in silence through the hospital like cleanliness of the hall.

"Just so you know," Eric says, a dark tone coming over his words. "I don't approve of mercenaries in my backyard."

"Harsh word. I prefer, freelancer."

"Whatever you call yourself, it's not welcome here. I owe Duggart a favor or two so I agreed to let Central and you into the N.U.S, and I'll help you get through the next checkpoint, but that's it. After that, you're on your own."

I nod. "Used to it."

That makes him stop. He turns to face me. "Be careful, Darcy. The guy you're after, he's not going to come lightly. This whole thing smells bad."

I sniff myself. "Weird, I showered this week,"

"It's not funny. You have no idea what you're walking into it."

"Yes I do," I tell him. "It's a party."

*

The main arcade of the N.U.S is covered by a dome. Most of the colony is underground, but here, in its uppermost real estate, you actually have a view, although it's not necessarily something you want to look at.

The dome is made of a latticework of steel and glass. Between the crisscross pattern, the huge globe of our home planet looms like a shadow. Once it was bright with lights in familiar patterns, countries and cities and coastlines. Now, it's dark. And in its center, a hole the size of a giant's fist. You can see stars through the hole, as if those distant suns and planets are laughing at the human folly that resulted in destroying our home.

There's an old saying about glass houses, but I don't remember how it goes.

The hall is busy with life. People stream between shops and down manicured fake-grass streets. There are signs pointing to various storefronts and offices and dozens of flags everywhere, remembrances of now-extinct States. There were a lot of states. I forgot most of their names.

On either side of the main hall are stepped rows of tiny apartments, many with small fake front yards. I think I hear some children playing. That's not something I hear much down below. I can't help but smile and think for a moment about what could have been, if...

I shake my head and continue down the long hall to clear glass partitions leading to the exclusive lofts above. Two guards stand near an elevator. One of them sees me first and fumbles for his weapon. I zoom in. The guards move in hilarious slow motion. I slide behind them and smack them both with my elbow in the back of the head. When the world returns to normal, they're on the floor but still awake. I grab the rifle from one of the dazed guards and press the button for the elevator.

"Hey!" shouts the guard. I turn and shoot him without looking and then turn my attention to the other one. My eyes are threats.

He drops his rifle and runs away as the elevator arrives.

I hate muzak.

I drop the rifle and kick it to a corner and take off my jacket. I tie it around my shoulders like it's a shawl.

When the elevator doors slide open, gentle piano music greets me like a friendly hug. A murmur of conversation, laughter, and clinking glass. The people are dressed in finery, gowns and suits and well-coiffed hair. I self-consciously rub some grit from my cheeks and smooth down my hair.

I remember my time in the New United States, after the fall of Earth and the establishment of the colony. It was nice, clean, but it wasn't like this.

I catch the eyes of the guests as I walk through. The men look me up and down without moving their head and the women make various shocked faces. I notice a few guys, muscles underneath their penguin suits, following me through the crowd.

Going unnoticed is not my style, apparently.

I take a breath and zoom in. The party guests are frozen, like a bad joke, while I rush past them. When I zoom out, I'm in the back of the large room at the base of a curved walkway. More muscles are coming down the walkway and the guys following me are on the way. I'm outnumbered.

Shit.

I untie my jacket and enter into a fighting stance.

"Stop," says a voice from the shadows. All the muscle guys freeze.

A figure emerges from the darkness in a sparkling white suit. He's got grey hair and a silver goatee. Aging skin that sags over hollow features, but every inch of him shouts gravitas. I recognize his face. Jacobson.

"There's no need for violence," he says softly. "I just want to talk."

I lower my arms. Just then his goons grab me and drag me towards the darkness.

✱

They've got my hands tied and two sets of man paws on my arms, otherwise I would have a fighting chance. They lead me down some darkened halls to an office, decked out in books and fake plants. The brutes shove me into a chair and Jacobson sits down across from me.

"Listen," I tell him, "I don't mind it rough, but at least buy me dinner first."

He smirks. "You always make jokes when you're nervous?"

I glance away, nonchalant. "I'm not nervous. Just hungry. I didn't get to eat at your fancy party."

He waves a dismissive hand at me. "We're not going to hurt you."

"So why are my hands tied?"

"For my protection, of course," he says. "I know what you can do. I know what you are, Darcy McAllister. I know *you*."

"Somehow I doubt all of those things."

He smiles like he's got something on me. I squirm a little in my seat, despite my usual swagger. My targets don't usually have a small army of security. Something *is* off about this whole thing.

"You don't remember me, do you?" he says. He rises from his chair and comes to stand close to me. "I can't imagine you do. It was a lifetime ago. But I remember everything."

He closes his eyes and his face takes on a kind of wistful repose. I can even see his nose twitch with scent memory.

He continues, "It was back on Earth. I was seven, maybe eight. You were older. Rebellious. Beautiful. It was a holiday on a house with a lake."

I remember the house. The back wall was all glass so you could see the water from every corner of the living room. There was a lot art in that house. And a young boy who followed me around like a loyal puppy.

When I open my eyes again, Jacobson has a hand outstretched to my cheek. "It's amazing," he says. "You're older than me and yet you look... twenty-five. Incredible." He shakes his head, eyes wide with awe. "How does it work?"

I test out the strength of the ties.

"Please, Darcy," Jacobson says returning to his big chair behind the big desk. "It doesn't have to get combative between us. I'm not interested in experimenting on you or anything like that." Here he laughs. "I'm an old man, and I'm fine with that. But just because I'm old, doesn't mean I don't dream of something better for my people."

"Which people? Americans? They seem to be doing fine up here while the rest of the human race scrapes to survive."

"I know and it makes me sad." He shakes his head again. "I don't mean just Americans. I mean people of all races and nationalities. This colony is unsustainable. You see it for yourself."

I stay silent, but I stop trying to force my way out of my restraints.

"You think this is the end of our story, of our species, but it's not. We have a future, just not here."

With a satisfied grin, Jacobson walks over to a panel and hits a button. Two shields begin to rise, revealing windows overlooking a large hangar bay. In the center, surrounded by machines and mechanics, a gleaming silver and white starship.

"Our future is out there," says Jacobson with a flourish. "And I want you to be a part of it, Darcy. There's just one thing, first…"

The ties on my wrists snap away just as the lights in the room turn off.

*

I wake up cheek down in my own blood. Cold, hard surface. Reminds me of college. I look up to see the steel bars of a jail cell. Yep, college.

A tall dark shape is nearby, saying something.

My ears are ringing and my vision is bloody and blurry. I shake off the dizziness and try to stand, but fail. Muscles crack and reset. My hearing returns, although muffled.

"Darcy?" says Eric Tamer, standing on the other side of the cell. "Darcy, are you okay? Can you hear me?"

"I can hear you," I croak. "Now shut up."

I push myself to a sitting position. I close my eyes. I zoom in and concentrate. I keep doing it until my muscles feel like I just got out of a massage. Sore, but working. When I open my eyes again, my audience has grown.

Eric is still there, his face pinched as if he's the one in pain. Jacobson is there, too, with a silly fucking grin and two of his muscle guys behind him.

"Amazing," he says as soon as I look up.

"Enjoyed the show?" I ask, standing up with more creaks and cracks. "I accept tips, by the way."

I focus on the muscled guys. They both have bruises on their faces and one of them is rubbing at his arm.

Jacobson notices my look and his Cheshire grin grows. "You held your own pretty damn well, even outnumbered. Put three of my guys in hospital." He steps closer to the bars. "Amazing," he says again.

"Hate to break it to you, gramps, but I don't date old men."

Tamer laughs. Jacobson's tone is still light, as if I'm not really in jail. Is everything a show with these guys?

"Would that I could keep up with you, my dear," says the old man. "But I have a better idea."

"Not interested," I say immediately.

Tamer shakes his head at me. "Just hear him out, Darcy."

I sigh, feigning boredom. "Fine."

Jacobson clears his throat. "You saw my ship. The mission is simple. Find the human race a new home. I want you on that ship. I *need* you on that ship. It will be a long journey and things may get tense aboard. Not to mention any *external* threats. We need someone with your skillset."

I nod at Eric Tamer. "Send him. He can take a punch."

Tamer responds, "I'm already going, D. I could use you on my team."

I turn back to Jacobson. "What's the compensation?"

The old man grins. "You will be paid very well."

I chuckle. "You should have led with that. My associate, Hurley, I'll want him to come too."

Jacobson turns to Tamer. "The pothead?" Tamer says. "Sure, if you say so."

The elder claps his hands together. "So we have a deal?"

I shake my head. "I'm still in a cell."

"Of course," Jacobson says and nods at Tamer, who opens the door with a wave of his wrist.

I stride out and find my brown leather jacket hanging nearby. I put it on, slowly, making a show. I turn to Jacobson. "So my warrant for you? It was all bullshit?"

He shrugs. "Think of it as a job interview. Captain Duggart is an old friend."

"Of course he is." I sigh. The offer is good. A chance to get off this godforsaken rock. A new adventure. Maybe a new world. Blue skies and trees and fresh air.

Tamer has a satisfied grin on his scarred face. "So what do you say, Darcy?"

I let myself smile for the first time in awhile. "Sounds like my kind of party."

Maybe there will be birds.

The Remembrance Engine

There was a string of endings that year that began my decline into madness. First, my father died and like God flicking a top, my world spun into chaos.

Drugs help soften the blow. After the government began decriminalizing drugs, enterprising dealers and innovative junkies experimented with volatile chemical cocktails. They likened themselves to the early explorers of the American continent: They searched for new horizons, new places to go, and new ways to imbue.

I got my chems from underground drug dens set up below the subway. These were like competing stores in a mall. Once down in the depths, there were flashy signs and pretty girls with tight skirts. They called out for my attention by jumping in front of me, bust-first, but I dodged them and found my favorite spot.

Inside, billowing fabric hid the walls and masked the sewer stench. Long couches arranged in star shapes had a few lounging ladies, smoking. Occasionally a man in a suit would be passed out. Go further into the den and you'll find its master, hidden in shadow. This place was ruled by a large black man in jeans and a vest that showed his muscles. His chair was custom-made, adorned with his namesakes twisted and curled into each other to form the legs and the arms. He went by the name Snake.

"You again." His voice had a deep rumble. As he spoke, he spat out of the side of his mouth. A long legged girl draped on his throne shifted to avoid the projectile. "Third time this week."

Snake smiled, but his words were also caked in judgment. In the shadows, I could make out his security. Huge guys with crew cuts and silhouette of rifles hidden in their trench coats.

I swallowed my prideful protest and nodded, "Yes, sir. It's been a tough month." My father had been in the ground for only a few weeks at this point. I kept his bible, always with him in those few last months, perched on my desk at home, a constant reminder.

Snake moved one of his muscled hands to squeeze the ass of the long legged girl by his side. She wore heavy makeup like a geisha. "Angel here will hook you up. Give the man a discount. He's our new best customer."

I followed the girl's ass to one of the bed-like couches in the far corner of the room. Each of the beds were connected via a series of wires and pumps to a repository at the heart of the star. The repository was a metal cylinder about the size of a beer keg. Inside was a mixture of chemicals that were unique to Snake and this establishment. I liked to imagine that he had a team of chemists working in a clean room next door with white doctor smocks and clipboards and computers.

Angel laid me down on the bed and stretched out my arms and legs. Like a flirtatious nurse, she ran her finger up my arm till she found a suitable vein. She punctured it with a needle she kept in her fingernail and inserted the chem tube into my body.

The high was immediate. It's important not to fall asleep otherwise you won't get your money's worth. It's equally important to stay alert, to focus on something physical in the world. I tried to find Angel in the sudden haze around me, but she was already gone. There was a candle nearby. It may have been tiny, a tea light, but from my sudden extreme senses, it looked massive, like a building on fire. I stared at the flickering colors and imagined myself inside that flame. I wasn't burning or dying, just living like that, constantly surrounded by fire. I couldn't cook hamburgers with my eyes, but if I tried to shake someone's hand, I would burn them.

My mind rattled around like this for a long time. I didn't think about my father. Time was impossible to parse, but I could feel when the high was subsiding. Most people hate this part, they much prefer the beginning when everything is weird and twisted and you feel so light inside, if you jumped into the air, you would float into space. But me, I liked the come down. I could feel my real self waking up while most of myself was somewhere nebulous. That was the sweet spot. One foot in, one foot out.

*

I met a girl. Not one of Snake's painted ladies, but another customer. We lay down at almost the same time in two adjacent beds. She smiled at me. She had strands of purple and pink in her black hair, thick black eyeliner and a deep red hue on her lips.

She whispered to me, "Hey, you believe in God?"

I started to answer.

"Don't answer that!" she snapped. "It was a trick question. If anyone asks you that, you say, 'None of your fucking business!' or-" here she took on a druggie intonation and massaged her veins, "'I only believe in this stuff.'"

"Okay," I said. She was funny. I liked that.

She said her name was Dess, as in You-Know-Who-Dess.

The rest of the night was a blur. In the morning, I woke in an unfamiliar bed with a snoring girl by my side. She was naked and facedown and on her back was a stylized version of Noah's Ark. Animals with thin smiles on their faces running out into the world, free of the confines of the ark. There were monkeys and elephants and hippos, all of them colorful and beautiful. I traced the lines of a Zebra with my finger.

Dess stirred and woke. She smiled at me.

"I don't remember much," I confessed. "What happened? Did we, uh, have sex?"

"Ouch," she said with a grin. She got up, revealing more tattoos down her legs. She slapped her ass and set the long legs of a giraffe dancing. "I think you'd remember."

I'm not so sure.

*

I lost my job (because business hours are for squares) and my highrise apartment.

I found a tiny apartment in a building full of older single guys, mostly divorcees. The rent wasn't much at all because it was the ugliest building in the city. I wrangled a custodial job at the Port Authority. They drug test, but you could buy clean piss across the street in an alley behind the deli.

It wasn't so bad. You're invisible in gray overalls behind a trash can on wheels. Nobody bothers you, not even supervisors. I liked it. Sometimes I'd find crumpled dollars on the floor. Everything went into my pocket and then, in the evenings, into my arm.

I was a fixture at Snake's. I even had my own couch, special just for me. Snake got out of his throne to show it to me. He said, "This," in that bass vibrato that seemed to shake the room, "is all you, my man." He clasped me on my shoulder in a gesture of friendship and comradery. Later, one of his girls gave me a handjob at the tail end of a high.

The chemicals that filled my body were different than any drug I experienced in my youth. They bonded with my white and red blood cells to create a new colored blood. Maybe green? I felt like if I sliced my wrist, a rainbow would emerge. And it wouldn't hurt. My body would heal itself because nothing could hurt me.

I wasn't the only one experiencing a change.

The Chem Craze, as coined by the evening news, spread like wildfire throughout the city. Violent clashes between dealers made the headlines daily. The rich set up private dens in converted penthouses. Restaurants became fronts, food in the front, chems in the back. I heard you could rent a limo with a working delivery system inside. They would drive you around the city while you flew through imaginary skies.

At the lower end of the spectrum, I saw the remnants of poor people drudge through the Port Authority to and from various seedy joints with chem bars in walk-in freezers and locked bathrooms. There seemed to be less people in the streets. The subways were deserted even in the middle of the day. Emptying trashcans across the massive complex, I saw people slumped over on benches and asleep on the floor. These weren't your average vagrants and bums, but young people in designer clothes and guys in suits using their briefcases as pillows.

Access to the underground was part of my new job. I had keys to those hidden access paths at the end of subway platforms and maps of the various underground layers beneath the city. I found a better way to Snake's place. No longer did I have to go through the chem mall with the pushers screaming for my attention. I simply opened a series of doors, first through the active train tunnels, then through the abandoned older system, and finally to one of the sewer tunnels. From there it was just a ten-minute jog through the darkness to Snake's.

I used a flashlight to avoid any major hazards along the way. I felt the excitement of my night at Snake's already coursing through my Vulcan-colored blood. I was almost running, but then I stopped suddenly, my senses alert at the sound of a footstep.

"Hey," said a familiar voice.

The voice emerged from the darkness. I shone my flashlight towards it.

It was Dess. She wore a tight black jumpsuit. Her hair looked unwashed and there were smudges of darkness on her skin and a faint odor of the sewer on her. She may have lived down here, homeless or, like me, she spent way too much time in the chem dens.

"I thought I'd find you here," she said. She sidled up close to me and cupped my ass. "Miss me?"

I couldn't remember when I had seen her last. "Sure," I said. "On your way to Snake's?"

"Actually," she said, "no. I'm heading somewhere else. Someplace new."

"New?"

"Different. Way different."

I looked into her eyes. She had that smoky-eye look where the eyeliner was thick as a picture frame. Inside the black border, her eyes were white as the cleanest teeth.

"Can I come?" I asked.

*

The first thing I thought when I saw it: It's so clean. Everything in this city is so dirty. Even when something isn't caked with dust, it's black from grease or red from rust. This thing was immaculate. Polished silver, windows as clear as can be, even the steel bolts shone a little in the light. It stretched back into the gloom, car after identical car. Like cleaning it was the hobby of a team of OCD janitors.

"It's a train," I said to Dess.

"Um, yeah. Duh." She shook her head and walked towards it.

We were in an aboveground station, somewhere in the wilds near the river. I could hear the lazy sounds of an active river, boat horns and seagulls and the gentle crashing of waves. The station looked like it had been abandoned for decades. The windows were broken and the steel beams above were exposed. On the ground was construction debris as if this place had been used as a warehouse and then forgotten.

Off in the farthest corner was the restored train. Where there was once a number or a letter was just a blank circle. The first few cars, with the clear windows, looked deserted. The last few had their windows tinted.

"Come on," she said, pulling at my arm. She helped me launch myself up a cinderblock step onto the train. Inside was as clean as the outside looked. The metal bars and chairs gleamed. The floor was almost reflective.

"This way," she said, leading me on.

We walked through the train, sliding open the doors between cars. I expected to hear the whoosh of movement every time we stepped between the cars, but there was only the silence of an ancient space. Finally, we reached a car with one of the tinted windows.

The smell of incense hit me first. Multiple varieties, stinking like a dorm room. There were a lot of people crowded into the train car, but they made almost no noise. No one talked above a whisper. Many looked to be sleeping. Dess tip-toed over them, holding onto the beams for support. I followed as best as I could but I stepped on some fingers and almost hit a girl with my knee. When I tried to say sorry, it was as if the whole car-load of people startled and quickly tried to drown me out with "Shhh!"s.

"Sorry," I said again, quieter this time.

I didn't see any chem cylinders or anyone looking like they were truly tripping. It just looked like a bunch of hippie kids on a train. I got nervous that there wasn't any chems at the end of this journey and my excitement from the tunnel seemed far away.

We reached the end of the crowded car without any major injury. I was preparing some choice words to say to my guide when she disappeared into the next car. I followed.

The car looked like a snow-covered forest. There were potted plants on the benches and astroturf on the floor. Everything was covered in that fake Christmas snow they sell in places like Florida. There was a teenager in the center of the car flicking tiny paper snowflakes into the air and some well-placed fans pushing them through the interior.

I found Dess sitting crosslegged on the floor near a huddle of bodies. They were moving slowly around each other. I couldn't tell if they were having sex or just playing a silent game of twister. I couldn't count the number of people, they were just a collection of arms and legs and hair.

Dess gestured with a nod for me to join her, which I did. I couldn't look away from the bacchanalia happening a few feet away. Occasionally I would glimpse a male's body, but I found I could focus on the female parts and it made for a pretty good show.

Finally, a head appeared. A woman's face emerged from the backdrop of bodies. She had long white hair and youthful features. She saw Dess and her face brightened. Using some force, she separated herself from the clutch of bodies and stood in front of us, naked and hairless. Dess rose to her feet and so did I, towering a good foot above them.

"Welcome back, dearie," she said to Dess, her voice all sugary and sweet. I could almost taste it like rosewater in the air. "I see you've brought a new friend."

Dess smiled and nodded. "He was on his way to Snake's."

"Ahhh," she said as if that said everything about me. She extended a hand, palm up as if in offering. "My name is Eve," and then she winked at me, "although that's not my real name."

I clasped her hand in mine not sure if I should shake it or kiss it. Instead I just held it tight for a few seconds. I said, "You can call me Adam."

"Perfect," said Eve as two more people emerged from the circle of bodies and produced a purple robe from somewhere on the floor. They draped the robe on top of Eve's body and tightened it without her help. Then they disappeared back into the menagerie.

I couldn't help myself any longer. "What exactly is going around here?" I asked her.

Eve started back towards the front of the car. Dess and I followed. She had an expression of sincere joy on her face, as if she was looking at a miracle.

"We offer a different kind of experience than what you're used to, Adam," said Eve as she caught one of the tiny paper snowflakes in her hand and studied it. She put the paper snowflake to her lips, kissed it, and then let it loose into the fake windstream of the train car. "When did you start using chems?"

I said nothing.

"It's okay," Eve continued. "You have nothing to be ashamed of. Not here. We understand what makes people partake in chems. We've all been there." Here she gestured at the crowded car behind us. "You want to forget. Right?"

I nodded.

"And have you forgotten?"

I hesitated. "I don't understand."

"The thing you were trying to forget. Did it work? Have you forgotten it?"

I thought about my father. It had been months now that he was gone, but images of his face, his withered body in a hospital bed came to me quickly. His voice over the phone. His words, "I'm dying," repeated over and over again. The frantic last-minute flight arrangements. The phone call on the way to the airport. The guilt.

"No," I told Eve.

I sat down, a sudden weariness in my body. Eve sat next to me, her lithe arms draped on my shoulders. "Of course," she whispered. "You can never forgot something that hurt you." Her breathe was hot in my ear. "There is a better way."

"Would you show me?" I asked.

Eve pulled away and sat up straight. "Kiss me," she said.

"What?"

Dess, sitting on the floor near us, leaped to her feet. "It's okay," she said. "Watch." She leaned into Eve and kissed her lips. It wasn't a long kiss. At the end of it, Dess licked her lips. Her eyes clouded and she almost lost her footing. The kid from the floor with the paper snowflakes was there in a flash to catch her and ease her onto the floor. He grinned at me.

"Your turn," said Eve.

I leaned in for a kiss. I thought, is this woman an angel? Is her blood mixed with chems? It was just the lipstick, I realized, as she used no tongue on our short kiss.

Immediately, I was caught in a memory. I was a child, bundled up, outside on a chilly morning. Trees were arranged in rows for as far as I could see. Sunlight drenched red apples, dozens per tree, hung only a short grab away. There were step-stools and ladders everywhere. I felt a comforting squeeze as my father lifted me to grab an apple. I laughed and so did he.

It was a sound I hadn't heard in so long. It seemed to echo in that make believe apple grove, a constant laughing loop.

When I snapped out of my high, I was in a pile of bodies in the first tinted car. I recalled other images: my father teaching me how to drive, watching movies on the couch, a football game in the freezing cold. But most of all, that laugh. I felt like if I could go back to that place, I would grab that laugh and hold onto it.

I'd never let go.

*

If my brain was a see-saw, it would be dizzy by now.

I became a regular at Eve's, but I still visited Snake's. I would remember during the week and then forget on the weekends. I was like an artist obsessing over a canvas, painting images and then scrubbing them out or a writer reworking drafts endlessly until the words become meaningless.

At work, I could just barely push my garbage can around. I moved in the slow meandering gait of the elderly or the apathetic. I only perked up in the evenings, on my way to the chem lounges.

One night, after sneaking through my secret custodial passageways, I found myself in the sewers, not sure which direction to go. Snake's was to the right and down another floor and Eve's was to the left and up an incline to the surface. I couldn't remember the day of the week or what I did yesterday. I lingered too long in the spot.

"Hey," said a deep voice from behind me.

Snake emerged from the darkness with some of his people, not the painted ladies from his den, but big guys like him. Security. They surrounded me. Snake towered over me.

"Where are you going?" he asked me.

"Your place, of course," I said. "I . . . I seem to have forgot the way."

"Right," he said, distracted. He looked closely at my shoulder. He reached out in what seemed like a friendly gesture, but then slapped my shoulder hard. A white powder flew off my Port Authority uniform. It wasn't dandruff, unfortunately.

"I know where you been, brother," said Snake. Two of his guys grabbed my uniform and lifted me up like I was nothing. Snake spat at floor and said, "That bitch been poaching my customers now for too long. Take me to her."

"I don't know what you're talking about!" I pleaded. "I'm loyal to you."

The guys dropped me. My knees hit the floor. Snake grabbed my shoulder and spun me around. "Bullshit. Now take me to her." I felt a pressure on the back of my head and the click of a gun.

"Okay," I said. "Okay."

I led them down through a series of tunnels to the inclined gangway and the abandoned station. I thought about leading them in the wrong directions, but I was too scared. I was a coward.

In the derelict station, Snake's guys pulled out automatic rifles that been hidden in their clothes. I stepped back into the shadows while they circled the stationery train.

Dess and I had coined a nickname for the train. We tried to come up with something majestic, like what you would name a castle or a spaceship. We settled on The Remembrance Engine because it sounded like a ride at a theme park.

Snake stood in front of the train like a boxer assessing his opponent. With only a nod of his head, his guys started firing rounds into the train. It sounded like a massive drill boring into the earth. The sound filled the old station and shook the construction equipment. When the drill subsided, I breathed a sigh of relief. But then the guys reloaded their rifles and started firing again.

I ducked behind some palettes and pressed my palms to my ears until it was over.

After a few minutes of silence, I found the courage to step out of hiding. Snake was staring at the train. He whispered to himself, "Thou shalt have no other Gods before me." He then looked at me, winked, and led his guys away.

The train looked like Swiss cheese that had been roasted. Smoke poured out of the hundreds of holes. There was a crackling of fire from inside. I couldn't hear any human sounds. I needed to see what I had done.

I used the cinderblock to hoist myself onto the train. It buckled a bit at my intrusion. The floor, once so immaculate, was littered with broken glass and splintered metal. I walked through the cars and braced myself before entering the first tinted car.

It was empty. I'd never seen it empty before. They must have gotten tipped off. I rushed through the car to Eve's wonderland, hoping to see the same thing. But I was disappointed.

The fake snow was covered in blood. Wisps of paper snowflakes still flew around the room from the one working fan. There were bodies strewn on the floor in startled positions like roadkill. I avoided stepping on them. I found Dess facedown on the metal floor. I reached down to check for a pulse like I'd seen on TV, but I couldn't. I shrunk back like she was made of fire.

I saw Eve in her purple robe on top of some of her people, like she had been trying to protect them. Her lips still sparkled but her skin was pale and she was bleeding from her chest.

I sat down next to her and held her chin in my fingers. I reached in to kiss those heavily chem-coated lips. Normally, she would stop after a moment or two but I kept the kiss going, the chems pouring into my mouth and flushing through my system like aggravated caffeine.

I pulled back, panting. The world shuddered as the train started moving. I could feel it dislodge from its resting place and it was suddenly flying through subway tunnels, picking up speed, then out into the surface. It rose above the tracks and flew into the air towards the sky.

And it never stopped.

All My Memories Are You

I wear your face to the party. It's not a costume party, but I don't care.

I admire a picture of you taped to the wall of my studio apartment. You are seated, legs crossed, looking back over your shoulder and laughing as if someone just said the funniest thing in the world.

I outline the sides of my mouth with a pencil and try to shape it just like yours. I look over my shoulder and laugh, my eyes on the mirror, mimicking you. Close, but not close enough. My nose is mousey, tiny, barely there. Yours is pronounced and proud. I use a bit of clay, glue, and foundation to match the bridge and nostrils. I remove my tiny silver glasses and reach for the contact lenses to match your hazy blue eyes.

There are more pictures of you on the wall, printed and taped, your face always half-titled away from the camera, your curly blond hair cascading down your back. You with a lip-sticked cigarette. You wearing heels and gold stockings. There's another version of you in full Goth, hair dyed metallic pink, black eye liner and lipstick. You are frowning. You always said you hate taking pictures. And yet there are enough pictures of you on social media for me to wallpaper my apartment with your face.

You like to joke that you can eat anything you want, but you are pencil-skinny while I look like one of those thick pens with multiple color options. I've had nothing but almonds and lemon water for weeks.

I found one of your favorite dresses from a few years back on eBay, it's black and white in a tent style. It was a special collection and cost more than I ever paid for a piece of clothing. I slide it on, careful not to pull on the sides.

I run a brush through my hair, a respectable replica.

I brought a half-dozen pictures of you to the salon. The stylist took a long time to admire your curls. "She's pretty," she said. "Who is she?"

I shrugged. "Some Australian actress."

The stylist made an *oooooh* sound and then proceeded to transform my stringy brown hair into a simulacrum of your natural look using extensions and lots of dye.

I spend hours on the makeup. It has to be right. It has to be you. My brushes and colors are arranged like a battlefield map in front of me. I study them like a general.

I imagine myself a great painter, not a Master, but one of those forgers who spends years creating a faux-Monet or Manet. There's talent in imitation.

✱

We met at camp.

You were one of the cool girls, stealing away into the woods to smoke clove cigarettes. I brought a stack of comic books taller than me. You held court in the wooden mess hall surrounded by girls who wore makeup and real bras. I would glance over my Batman graphic novel at you and every once in a while, I thought I saw you glance back, as if you were reading the titles. As if you were interested.

At the end of the summer, I was walking through the woods alone, as usual, on the outskirts of the camp.

"Hey," said a high voice. You were sitting cross-legged on a boulder, puffing on a cigarette. "Jessica, right?"

I adjusted my glasses, big purple frames, too big for my adolescent face. *She knew my name.*

"Yeah," I said, feigning nonchalance.

"I could use a favor." You tossed the cigarette, still lit, into the woods, and stood up. You were taller than me by just a few inches, yet you towered. It was so strange to see you up close, like meeting a celebrity you only knew from TV.

You started walking back to camp. I followed. "I'm Brianna," you said, "but you can call me Bri."

We stopped at a ramshackle shed, no windows, near the soccer field. You lowered your voice.

"There's a boy in there," you whispered. "He's waiting for me. He says he loves me, but he's a liar." You tossed back you hair then, your signature move. "He says even in the dark, he would recognize me. Let's find out."

You grasped my shoulders and spun me towards the shed. Your breath was hot and sweet in my ear. "If he asks, you are Bri. Okay?"

"Okay," I said.

You see, you started it.

*

All your fingers are slim and pretty. Except one.

You injured it during a volleyball match. I was there, in the stands. You screamed as you hit the ball with your manicured fingers outstretched. You collapsed onto the gym floor and your teammates flocked to you. The audience cheered when you got up and brushed away the concerns of your teammates and kept playing. It was a high stakes match, after all, and you are committed.

Only after your team won did you go to the hospital. By then it was too late. Your finger would be curved, witch-like, forever. As a joke, you dressed like a witch the next Halloween. Everyone loved it.

I used a hammer.

I went to the hospital just to get the drugs. The nurses were incredulous.

"How did this happen?" they asked.

"I got it"—wince—"stuck in a doorframe."

They put my finger in a little splint and sent me away. As soon as I got outside, I popped an oxy and then ripped up the splint and left the tape and stick and gauze on the sidewalk.

I'm committed, too.

*

The party waits inside. I reach for it with my gnarled-fingered-hand and pull it back, worried the pain might crack a layer in my makeup.

There's a mirror by the door. One last check of my face. It's perfect. It should be, it's yours. I studied your makeup tutorials online. You have a gift for it, an artist's eye. Did you notice the ticker counting up how many times someone watched your videos? That was me.

I grip the handle with my non-dominant hand and push it open.

I expect fanfare when I walk through the door. I always assumed whenever you enter a room, there is applause, like one of those old

TV shows with a live audience. Or at the very least, some reaction. But the scattered guests in the low lit foyer barely look up at my presence. One girl, lonely in the corner, perks up. I don't make eye contact. I toss back my hair like I'd seen you do a million times. Then I stride through the room as if I'm a queen and this is my fiefdom.

Now they're looking.

*

The next time I pretended to be you, it was years later. We were juniors in high school.

There was a rumor going around school that you gave a sophomore a blow job. The kid, Ryan something-or-other, already had a reputation before this. He had sandy brown hair, blue eyes, played on the basketball team, and was renowned in the boy's locker for being "big."

The junior and senior girls whispered about him as he passed in the halls, throwing a basketball over the heads of all the shorter kids.

"Look at him," they whispered. "He's big everywhere else. It's got to be true."

I was often in school late into the afternoon with my clubs (chess, A/V, math) or helping one the teachers decorate the halls. I heard the scrape of shoes in the gym like a practicing symphony. Every once in a while, a grunt, a curse, or a shout.

When practice was done, twenty sweaty boys crashed through the big gym doors to the nearby locker room. The smell should have been noxious, but I found it intoxicating. It was like a scent memory, but I didn't know from when or where.

I was helping a teacher decorate a huge sign, but she got a phone call and had to go, muttering something about her 'useless husband.'

After she left, the parade of basketball boys made their way out of the locker room. I counted. Amazingly, he didn't come out. I put down my glitter pens and brushes and walked over to the locker room door.

Feeling brave, I pushed open the door. That same musky, almost moldy, smell. I breathed it in. It gave me strength.

He was wearing a towel around his waist and earbuds in his ears, oblivious to the world. His back and chest had those hard lines you see on movie stars.

After what felt like ten minutes, he noticed me, started, and reached up for his earbuds.

"Hey," he said, "you shouldn't be in here."

I ignored that. "I heard about you and Briana."

His eyes flashed downwards. "Oh. Right. Are you her friend?"

"Yes," I lied.

"Look. I don't know how that rumor started. My friends and I were just joking around, and, well, I don't know, maybe, I, uh.."

As he was babbling, I didn't stop walking towards him. Who was this brazen person? I was you. I was your soul in my body.

I got so close to him, I could see the condensation on his chest. He didn't smell musky or sweaty. He smelled sweet like soap. I reached for his towel and let it drop. I touched him and he shuddered.

"What's your name?" he asked.

"Call me Bri," I said.

*

Back at the party, people are starting to notice.

"Hey Brianna!" someone shouts. She's a black girl holding a plastic wine cup, a frizzy pink drink within. I try to hide my smile as she motions me over.

"I thought you were travelling," she says at a conspiratorial whisper, "what are you doing here?"

Mimicking your cadence took some time and patience. Thankfully, I've had a lifetime of practice.

I release an exasperated breath. "So much drama," I tell the girl. "Family stuff."

She nods in a knowing way.

I pretend someone is calling me. I touch the girl's shoulder with my bad finger and say, "I'll be back."

She goes back to her frizzy drink.

I'm so happy, I could scream.

*

In college, we became friends.

To be clear, I didn't follow you. I got into a bunch of schools. You got that ridiculous volleyball scholarship. My mom wanted me close, though, so when I found out you were going to a nearby school, it may have swayed my decision.

Of course, I wasn't in your orbit so you didn't see me. I was like lonely Pluto, status-stricken, floating far away from the more popular planets.

But I am fastidious. I manufactured a meeting, a literal collusion.

You used to ride your multi-colored fixie around campus. Your tall body looked like it hovered on the thin frame of the bike, but you rode so fast, it was sheer will and gravity that you kept vertical. You rode with your characteristic laissez-faire attitude, barely acknowledging the pedestrians.

That is, until you hit a bookish girl with stringy brown hair, a mousey nose, and small silver glasses.

"Oh my god!" you shout and launch yourself at me, your bike forgotten in the grass beside the path. "Are you okay?"

You reach out your hand and I grasp it. It feels so weird to touch you. I am dizzy, dark spots in the glare from the sun. "I'm sorry, I—, uh—, I must not have been looking."

"No," you said. "It was my fault. I'm so sorry." You remove your sunglasses to get a better look at my face. "Hey, didn't we go to high school together?"

I smile. "Yeah, I think so. I'm Jessica."

The tension in your shoulders relaxes as I get up and stretch, unhurt. "I'm Brianna. Bri."

I nod. "I remember." You help me gather my scattered belongings.

"Hey," you said, "Can I buy you a coffee or something? I feel bad. Do you have time?"

"I have time."

After that, we were inseparable for awhile. We bonded over Arcade Fire and Heath Ledger's The Joker. He was so crazy, it was sexy as fuck. We would quote his breathy, marble-mouthed lines to each other and try to get his laugh right.

You brought me into your friend group. Some of the other girls were suspicious (they were not wrong), but they kept quiet—as far as I knew—because we were such fast friends.

You were rambunctious and rebellious. A sweet supplicant to the teachers, but a wild woman in the night time. We broke into campus buildings afterhours to hang out on rooftops, drink vodka and smoke weed. There was always a small crowd to attend to you, girls and boys ready to jump when you said so.

For awhile, I was glad to be a hanger-on, a follower in your wide shadow. But, maybe I wanted too much.

It started with your ex-boyfriends. You had so many of them, they were like candy wrappers discarded on the sidewalk in your wake. It wasn't hard to find them, pick them up, and let them inside me.

Then it was your current boyfriend, once or twice, while you were busy studying. I didn't think you'd care too much, honestly, it was just a boy.

You accused me of it and I denied it. But your friends had evidence and the boy did not deny it.

I think it was the lie, ultimately, that offended you. If I had admitted it, maybe you would have just dumped the dude and we'd stay friends.

You told me once, boys are liars, but they're not the only ones.

*

At the party, things are getting livelier.

Dozens more people have showed up so that the apartment feels cramped and small. Sweaty. I go into the bathroom to check my makeup and dab at the wetness on my cheeks and forehead.

When I come out, a few girls waiting in the bathroom line start whispering and giggling. I glare at them and brush past without a word.

But then it happens again as I'm walking through the crowded kitchen to get another drink. Whispers, laughs.

I march towards them, ready to fight, when I catch a reflection in the shiny glass of the eye-level microwave. I turn and you're there. Somehow. Not in Europe or some mythical foreign land. Right here, in this crowded kitchen. My double.

You are wearing a sleeveless blouse and way too casual jeans. Looks like you got a haircut recently too, a trim that scales back your curls to just under your shoulders. I don't like it.

"*Jessica*," you say, hissing the constants in my name like a curse. "What are you doing?"

I grin at you, but you respond with a nasty snarl. Everyone in the kitchen, and in the adjoining rooms, is staring at us.

"That's not my name," I say.

And then I laugh in a perfect imitation of our favorite Joker, high and loud and wild.

A Fiery Lull

Dear Maria,

I set the field aflame. Again. Third time in three years.

First, it was locusts. They came from the south as a murmuration, huge and curved into the shape of an evil grin. They descended on my crops, ate and ate their bodyweights and more. I had no choice, but to burn them out. We surrounded the fields with flamethrowers, killing everything in our path, plant and bug, native and invader.

Next, it was the *federales*. They got wind of some of my unusual strains and were on their way to investigate. Like the insects before them, they swarmed in black vans, kicking up a dust-storm behind them. I gave the signal to burn the fields and even my precious incubator plants.

And now, it's the latest cartel war budding up against my business. I am not associated with any one family, so I'm in the middle of it, a victim of the violent winds that pass through the country like a traveling tropical storm.

We are packing up to leave to America. Etain is here with me. She misses you. You would be surprised at how big she's gotten! Even picking her up is getting difficult for this old man. She's holding the doll you gave her, with the red hair, like her momma when I first met you.

I turned your old studio into my office. Your artwork still hangs on the walls, the glazing glowing red from the fires. We're watching through the big windows as fieldhands burn my life's work.

I hope they are giving you my letters. Please know that though we are leaving the country, we will be back for you. When things quiet down. When it's safe.

I promise, Maria. I will come back for you.

Te amo, mi vida.

—Jorge.

*

(Scrawled across a billboard near East Hampton, NY)
TO SLEEP, PERCHANCE TO DREAM.

✱

Yo bro! Check this out.

I was working a quad shift at the farm. You wouldn't even recognize the place. You worked a summer here, like, what, five years ago? We've got three huge greenhouses now. The boss named them after those famous ships, the Nina, the Pinta, and the—uh—I don't remember the last one. Besides, he doesn't let anyone in that one.

So, I'm doing my usual work: Assessing every new flowering plant, making notes about size and color. The rows are endless, green aisles like trees along a highway. Small plants at the front and larger, thicker ones by the back. It takes me half a day to do one row.

Suddenly, there's a whisper beside me. I startle and almost drop my tablet.

"Hey," she says again.

It's the boss's daughter. You remember her, right? She was a little stick of a girl at fifteen. Well, she looks a lot different now. She had on a runner's outfit, a tight crop top and even tighter pants. Her legs seemed to go up to her chest and her hair was tied into a ponytail, it snaked down her back like a tattoo.

You know me, bro, I fall in love easily.

"Hi," I said.

She stepped further out of the shadows. She was wearing inky black so she still blended. She came close to me. "I need your help," she whispered.

"What—what can I do?" I stammered.

"I want to do something bad," she said.

I felt myself stiffen. Maybe love wasn't the right word.

She grasped my hand and started leading me away. "Um, but, I, uh, I have to work!" I protested for some stupid reason.

She just laughed and opened a nearby service door. "It's okay," she said, "I know your boss."

Outside, it was night, but stadium lights created an artificial day. As usual, the farm was abuzz with activity, but the other people were far away or engrossed in their duties.

The girl led me through the shadows of the bright light beyond the dome of the Nina to hug the walls of the Pinta. I could hear the machinery in there, churning along 24/7. The flower was converted to other forms in there: heated oils, crystalline wax, or distilled liquids for tinctures.

"Where are we going?" I whispered.

"Come on!" she replied.

We were exposed for a few minutes while we ran towards the next greenhouse, the one marked S/M. She found another darkened corner and we were hidden again. The building looked bigger and more imposing up close. We were both breathing heavy from the run. She had a wild, expectant, look on her face.

She pressed a button and a door revealed itself from the blank wall. Then she punched in a code and the door hissed opened. She grasped my hand and pulled me forward. The door slid shut behind us.

Inside was a laboratory, of sorts. It was similar to the greenhouse where I worked, but even at a glance, I knew the flowers were different. The strains were—I'm not sure how to describe it—unique. There were alien-like purple flowers, stalks and buds that glowed neon green, a few were an unsettling dark blue, while others looked a natural green, but when I looked closer, they had thorns where they shouldn't or had strange colorful patterns.

"What is this place?" I asked, awed.

She took a moment to let it all sink in. "Experimental strains. My father's life's work."

I crashed landed back to reality. I started to back away. "I shouldn't be in here," I said. "We should go."

I turned away. That's when she kissed me.

"Julien," she said. I didn't know she knew my name. She made it sound exotic, European. "Please stay."

I swallowed and nodded. She smiled and leaned in for another kiss, a peck on my cheek. Then she turned on her heel and started wandering among the strange plants. At various places, random as far as I could tell, she picked off a flowering bud and then went back to searching. At one point, she went back and grabbed a bit more from two bright green plants with orange hairs.

Finally satisfied, she ducked away from the rows of plants to a kind of maintenance area. There was a ladder to a loft. She went up first. I tried not to stare.

The loft was small, but furnished. A couple of couches, a few screens mounted to the walls. A bookshelf.

She sat down on a couch and beckoned me to sit next to her. On the little table in front of the couch, she laid down the buds she had collected. Their multi-colored hues looked rainbow-eqsue. She used the bottom of her palm to start crushing the buds, mixing them together.

She broke the silence. "Have you heard of Lull?"

"No," I said quickly.

"Liar," she grinned.

I sighed. "I have heard of it, but it's dangerous. I think. Doesn't it make you . . ."

"Yes," she said. "Or so I've heard. I've never tried it before."

I had a bad feeling about all of this, but what was I supposed to do at this point?

I asked, "How do you make it?"

As she crushed more of the flower, she said, "It's a cocktail. A blend. Different strains, combined in the right amounts. I've been researching, for awhile. I think this should do it."

She finished crushing all the flower and started rolling a joint from the crumbs.

I gulped. "I don't know if I want to, you know, do that."

She laughed. "It's not for you. It's for me. I wanted someone else here to, I don't know, just to make sure nothing goes wrong."

"Like if you stop breathing or something?"

"Or something."

She used her tongue to seal the joint and took a moment to admire it. It was thick like a baby banana. She rummaged around the table until she found a lighter. She lit the joint, took a long drag, and sat back. Her eyes were closed already and she said in a kind of contemplative tone, "You ever just want it all to stop?"

And then she fell asleep.

*

ZERO STARS!!

I rarely write reviews, but I feel compelled after your RUDE employees treated my friends and I like garbage last night.

It was my best friend's birthday. We arrived around 2 A.M., already tipsy from the drive over. As soon as the doors swooshed open, we were elated. The place was packed with beautiful people, dancers hovering in the sky, and those interactive projection things—I love those!

The hostess floated in to greet us looking like some kind of goddess. She wore a long flowing green dress, with a wide slit in the front, a little too much skin in my opinion, but she pulled it off. She introduced herself, but it was hard to hear over the pounding music. I think she said her name was Elaine.

Anyway, it started off great. As she took us through the winding pathways of the club to our table, maybe-Elaine smiled and chatted with my best friend. Projection-butterflies came at her command to rest on her manicured fingers. Then she pointed at one of us and the butterfly came to rest on our shoulders or top of our head.

But then things took a turn once we sat down. We ordered a few bottles, a few thousand dollars' worth, just to start! Then your hostess leaned in to me and tried to sell me some "designer cannabis strains."

I said, "Bitch, I don't smoke that street rat stank."

Well, I guess she didn't like that. Even though, what's that phrase, the customer is always right—especially the customer who just dropped a few thousand dollars.

As soon as I refused her under the table deal, she got rude and insulting. I saw her talking to some of the waitresses and looking in our direction. We were practically IGNORED all night and I know it was because of her.

I complained to the manager and I saw him talking to her later that night, there was shouting and some wild gesturing, although I couldn't hear what they were saying. I hope she got fired.

Even if she did, I won't be back to your club and neither will any of my friends until you hire NON-RUDE employees.

✷

(Spotted on a billboard outside Albany, NY)
WE WERE MEANT TO SLEEP.

✷

Dear Maria,

I'm sorry it's been so long since my last letter.

I've never lied to you. So, I need to tell you, it's been tough, lately, with Etain.

She is unable to keep a job and she keeps getting into trouble in the city. As a teenager, she was rebellious and mischievous. I was the same way. Heaven knows I was a terror for my poor madre until I met you and settled down. I have tried to be understanding and forgiving with her, but she tests me. Whenever she is home, we fight. She blames me for her mother not being around. She is starting to hate me, I fear.

I don't know how much longer I can keep the lie from her.

In happier news, Etain has taken a liking to one of the field hands at the farm. He's not a lowlife like her usual boyfriends – he wouldn't be working for me if he was – but he has a big mouth. Always texting some brother who lives in another state. A little too chatty, in my opinion. But she seems happy.

Although she doesn't need the money, I have insisted that Etain hold a job in addition to her studies so she can learn responsibility, just like we did. She's still trying to find the right fit.

I will write again soon.

Te amo,

—Jorge.

*

hey bro. I think I have a girlfriend. Etain, aka the Bosses' Daughter, likes to hang around the employee's hut waiting for my shifts to end. I get some weird looks from my co-workers, but I don't care.

She usually looks like she is the middle of a workout, all skin and sweat. But not tonight. She is wearing what may have been a chiffon gown years ago, but full of rips and tears, like a Halloween costume. Her hair was half-done up one side and stringy and down on the other. Her makeup was similarly half-done, as if she got bored with the whole thing in the middle.

"Hi," I said when I saw her. She was sipping on a vape. The clouds that surrounded her were a maelstrom of colors. "You look nice. Are you going to a party?"

"We," she said grasping my hand like she does, "are going to a party."

She wrinkled her nose in that way that may be considered rude to most people, but doesn't bother me. "You'll need a shower and a change of clothes."

She smiled wide at the prospect and then took off at a run towards the big house. I followed after her. The house was massive and textured in glass. I'd never been inside the house before, even after working here all these years.

It was, as expected, garish and loud. Artwork on every wall, sculptures in every corner. Massive chairs flown in from Northern Europe, it looked like they still had some snow on them. I tried to stop, to gawk like a gallery-viewer, but Etain yanked my arm and led me up the stairs to her suite.

She had three rooms all to herself, each one larger than the next. Her closet was the size of my apartment with seating and lighted mirrors.

"I grabbed some of my dad's old clothes, back when he was a bit . . ." *she made a squeezing gesture with her hands.* "Younger."

And then she laughed in such a cute way, I felt my heart pulse.

An hour later, I emerged wearing a button down shirt, slacks, and a belt that squeezed the life out of my stomach. We got high and then went downstairs to the waiting car.

In the backseat, on the drive to the city, Etain was calm, as always, but I was a ball of nerves.

"Are we going to be late?" *I asked her.*

She smiled and slid open a compartment between us. There was a grey satchel inside. She patted it like a dog.

"Hard to be late when we're bringing the party."

Oh.

She saw my discomfort. "Are you nervous?"

"A little."

"Don't be. It's . . . hard to describe. But wonderful, in its own way."

I remembered the lectures in health class. "Isn't it like death? Like you die for a few hours?"

She laughed. "Not at all! There are these amazing images. Like you are watching a movie of yourself. Or you are experiencing something from a different perspective."

"Different how?" *I asked.*

"You'll see."

She leaned back and sighed, as if she had already taken some of the Lull. I watched the rise and fall of her chest and lingered on the exposed bits of skin beneath the tattered dress. I was used to seeing her in more relaxed attire. Dressed up as she was, it was like she was a completely different person.

The car pulled up to a high rise and a doorman opened the door for us. I half expected paparazzi, but there was only the busy background chatter of the city.

Her heels clicked against the marble floor of the hallway as she led me towards an elevator. Not surprisingly, she pressed the button for the top floor.

The door opened directly into a penthouse apartment. There were floor to ceiling windows overlooking a bustling night-time metropolis. In the daytime, it's probably flooded with light. But tonight it's all shadows. Even the big chandeliers and floor scones are set to a dim. Sheets hang from the high ceiling, forcing us to push our way through the apartment as if we're under colorful water.

We emerged from the hall to a large living area. Guests, similarly dressed in finery, but somehow damaged or weathered a bit, called out to Etain. She manufactured a wide smile, the brightest I've ever seen on her, before she embraced them. She introduced me, but I didn't catch any of the names.

Etain unveiled the grey satchel from behind her back and the other guests tittered and smiled at her. The hostess, obvious in her pristine gown and impossible heels, separated herself from the gaggle. She fake-smiled at me and then leaned into Etain and whispered, "Wait till you see the Den."

We all followed her down another hall to a bedroom which looked like about the half size of one of the greenhouses. There were blankets and pillows piled up in mazes and cul-de-sacs. Beds lined the walls, more than I've ever seen in one place.

"It's perfect," Etain whispered. She was glowing, excited. I couldn't help it, I was excited too.

In the center of the room were three massive vaporizers. Etain went to study them. The little gaggle of women dispersed expect for the hostess, who hung back next to me. She was a foot taller than me in those heels.

"So you're the new boyfriend?" she said to me with a side-long look. "Must be a special person to keep her interested."
There was malice in her tone. Something else, as well. She gave me a weak smile and walked over to Etain. She put her hands on Etain's waist and pulled her closer to her, an obviously intimate gesture. They both laughed.
I wandered the corners of the large room, smiling at the beautiful strangers. I overheard one woman lean into her friends and say, "I read some people used to do it in the middle of the day."
One of the ladies gasped. Another one exclaimed, "How uncouth!"
From the center of the room, the hostess called out, "Everyone find someplace comfortable."
There were more titterings and nervous whispers from the crowd. Etain swung the grey satchel around and started loading the Lull into the vaporizers. They started to emit a mist into the room. It was thick and white like snow.
Etain smiled at me before she was engulfed in the storm.
See you on the other side, bro.

*

Sleep
From Wikipedia, the free encyclopedia
This article is about sleep in humans. For other uses, see Sleep (disambiguation).

For centuries, mankind has relinquished half of their lives to somnolence. In the mid 21st century, spurred by the Accelerated Evolution Movement, or AEM, which was the scientific movement to reach humanity's evolutionary goals through technology and bio-engineering, sleep became a target. Politicians ran on a campaign of radical change. Without sleep, they argued, how much more could we accomplish? They poured billions in AEM research facilities until a "cure" was found. A combination of drugs delivered to five year old children through a year of micro-doses tweaked their bio-chemistry so that sleep became, after a single generation, eradicated. Some countries banned it completely while most societies frowned upon it, asking instead, What would you do if you had half of your life back?

✻

[static]
"Dispatch, dispatch, reports of active blaze on 66th St. and Amsterdam. Penthouse. Engines en route."
[static]

✻

(Photographed on a billboard near New Platz, NY)
I WISH I KNEW YOU.

✻

Dear Maria,

There has been an incident.

Don't worry, Etain is fine. But some of her friends have died, including her boyfriend, Julien. There was a fire at a party they attended in Manhattan. Apparently, they were *sleeping* at the party. There was an open flame somehow that caught fire, we don't know how yet. The police have been around a few times now, asking questions. They seem to think Etain is responsible.

She didn't come home for days and then she appeared one night in my study.

Once I made sure she was fine, I demanded answers and asked her why the police were asking questions about her and her experience with *sleep*.

We had an argument. Our worst yet. She brought you up, accused me of taking away the only person who ever truly loved her.

I had no choice, I had to tell her the truth. About that day, in the old farmhouse, when she was a baby. About the fire you started.

I will never understand how you left her alone in the house. What would have happened if I came home a little later? I couldn't risk something like that happening again. I had no other choice.

I told Etain everything, finally.

Tears streamed from her eyes, but she was stone-faced, like polished steel.

"I don't believe you," she said.

"You're a liar!" she shouted.
I shouted something back.
Then she ran. Out of the room and out of the house. I don't know where she went or if she'll be back.
—Jorge.

*

Official transcript of podcast "Mysteries of New York," Episode 16

[ominous musical intro]
SC: *Hello and welcome to the episode 16 of the "Mysteries of New York" podcast where we discuss mysterious occurrences in New York state. I'm your host, Samantha Cunning, with my co-host, Darius White. How are you doing today, Darius? Staying warm?*
DW: *Trying to, Sam, but it's not working. We're looking at single digit temps for the rest of the week here in Buffalo.*
SC: *Brr. Let's get right to today's topic. A topical one, a news story that is getting a lot of play throughout the national outlets.*
DW: *Although it is very much a New York kind of story, wouldn't you agree?*
SC: *Definitely, Darius. And what are we even talking about? The billboards, of course.*
DW: *Yes. The Poet of Poughkeepsie.*
SC: *So named because of the first spotting of the billboard on a state road outside the city. We only have one picture of that sighting before county officials painted over it. The picture was taken in a foggy winter morning and obscured most of the text. But the style was unmistakable.*
DW: *Especially when similar fragments in thick black spray paint started showing up on the highways and roads of Long Island and then upstate. This was about six or seven months ago, isn't that right, Sam?*
SC: *Yeah, that sounds right. It was a news-worthy story almost immediately. There was a whole group of photographers who*

roamed the roads looking for new fragments.
DW: Before authorities could burn them down.
SC: That's right. A few weeks after the first fragment was painted over by local authorities', other municipalities around the state started doing the same thing. But after every washing over, the fragment would re-appear as if by magic. So, they started taking more violent action. Was it the same person, working tirelessly through the days and nights to re-do his or her work, or was it copycats, fans, or maybe it was some kind of collective?
DW: No one knows for sure, although there have been a lot of speculation about the Poet's identity and motivation.
SC: It was the substance of the words that angered the local governments. The fragments were about sleep. The joy of rest. The lost magic of dreams.
DW: We both can attest to years of demonization of sleep, first in school, then from politicians, business owners, etc.
SC: And that's what scared them.
DW: Yes. They burned the billboards so the fragments could not be redone. It was not uncommon to drive down a highway in New York and see a seemingly endless row of burning billboards.
SC: But who is the poet of Poughkeepsie and what are they after? What is their goal?
DW: We'll dig into that more after a short message from our sponsor.

*

Maria,

They're allowing me one last letter. Maybe I should have called? We haven't spoken in so many years, I don't know if I even remember the sound of your voice.

I've been arrested on federal charges. It was Etain. She was using a cocktail of my strains to jerry-rig a sleep inducer. The FBI has hundreds of texts from Etain's boyfriend detailing how she manufactured the drug and brought it to the apartment where those kids died. Even if she didn't start the fire, they are blaming her for what happened.

I swear, I didn't know what she was doing. I would have stopped it if I knew.

Of course, the Feds don't believe me. They are sending me away. She'll be on her own now. Maybe she always was.

In the end, I was a liar. I never came back for you.

Good intentions too often turn into broken promises.

Lo siento, mi amor.

Goodbye, Maria.

*

r/newyorkstate—Posted by u/SheDidn'tDoIt six days ago
[MEGATHREAD] FRAGMENTS

okay, guys, this is it! I've asked the mods to close down all the other sightings threads so we can keep it all in one place.

It won't be long now. State police have closed down all roads and exits out of the state. Federal authorities are going door to door. New York is locked down and it's going to stay that way until the Poet is caught.

It's our last chance to help her get her message out. With the enhanced scrutiny, sightings have been rare, but they're out there. Billboards are being monitored so we're starting to see pieces of her last poem on motel signs, drive thru windows, behind Costco's, in gas station bathroom mirrors, wherever they are, WE HAVE TO FIND THEM.

Remember: Every drawing has a nearby number. Put those numbers in sequence and we have the order. Then it's just a matter of finding all the fragments. Good luck, guys!

EDIT #1: We are over halfway there!

EDIT #2: Have you guys gotten any weird home visits lately? Like, from the FBI? At first I thought it was a prank, but then they got all mad at me when I wouldn't let them in. They threatened to arrest me, but then I let them search my house and they were satisfied, I guess? They said they might be back.

EDIT #3: I think we should stop.

✸

(Published on the front page of *The New York Times*)

When I sleep,
I dream of my mother.
My mother I never knew.
My mother who tried to kill me.
Flames
Have followed me my entire life.
When I close my eyes,
I let them take me.

Burn me this time.
I'm ready.

Acknowledgments

First and foremost, I want to thank my amazing wife, Shawn, for believing in me and encouraging me and being not just an amazing wife but my best friend. I love you, Shawn!

To my "fantasy world" (aka author) friends, thank you for sharing, commenting, critiquing and helping me get my stories out in the world.

To my family and "real world" friends, thank you for being in my life. I love each and every one of you.

To my daughter, Emilia, thank you for being my greatest inspiration.

Bibliography

- "Ophelia and the Beast" first appeared in the chapbook, *Rabid Transit* in 2003; reprinted in the folk-lore themed online magazine, *Truancy*, in 2019.
- "A Beauty, Sleeping" was published in the online magazine, *The Fortean Bureau* (2004).
- "Halfway Down the Hole" was published in the online literary magazine, *pindeldyboz*, in 2005 and reprinted in 2021 in the online horror magazine, *Not Deer Magazine*.
- "Rapunzel Goes Mad" was also published by *pindeldyboz* in 2005.
- "Doll Parts" is original to this collection.
- "Number One Hit" was published in the fifth issue of *Interfictions Online* and then reprinted on the podcast *StarShipSofa* in 2019.
- "Do What You Desire" was first published in the sixth issue of the print zine, *Say . . .* from Fortress of Worlds and reprinted online at *Strange Constellations* in 2019.
- "The Conductor Sighs" was first published in the email newsletter *Flash in a Flash* and then reprinted from the same publisher in a print anthology *Worth 1,000 Words: 101 Flash Fiction Stories by 101 Authors*.
- "Time Keep" was published in *Fission #1* by the British Science Fiction Association (2021).
- "It Only Rains At Night" was published online by *Strange Constellations* in 2019.
- "D" is original to this collection. It was written during Clarion.
- "Bee Mine" was published by the literary magazine *Your Dream Journal* (2019).
- "Stay In Your Homes" was published in the long running print magazine, *Space and Time Magazine*, in their 137th issue, in 2020.
- "But My Heart Keeps Watching" was published in *Underland Arcana #8* (2022) by Underland Press.
- "Never Stop Moving" is original to this collection.

- "The Dying Disease" was published online at *Literally Stories* (2021).
- "Young Man, Are You Lost?" was published by *The Night's End Podcast* (2021).
- "Life In A Glasshouse" was published in the anthology, *No Ordinary Mortals*, by Rogue Blade Entertainment (2022).
- "The Remembrance Engine" was published online at *Penumbric Speculative Fiction Magazine* (2022).
- "All My Memories Are You" was published online in the *DISGUISE* issue of literary magazine, *perhappened* (2021).
- "A Fiery Lull" was published in *Underland Arcana* #10 (2023).

Biography

Elad Haber has been quietly publishing short fiction for more than twenty years. He attended Clarion when he was just eighteen years old. You might find his words in various forgotten corners of the Internet or in the dusty backrooms of basement bookstores.

His stories have been featured in magazines such as *Interfictions Online, pindelyboz, StarShipSofa, Space & Time Magazine, Lightspeed, the Simultaneous Times Podcast,* and *Underland Arcana.*

Visit eladhaber.com for links and news.

Printed in the USA
CPSIA information can be obtained
at www.ICGtesting.com
LVHW040725090724
784970LV00007B/115